a Songbird novel

geronimo

MELISSA PEARL

ISBN: 153693772X
ISBN-13: 978-1536937725

NOTE

For previous Songbird Novels, I have placed the playlist here, but one reader suggested to me that I should put it in the back, as the song list can give too much away. So that's what I've done. If you'd like to see it first, you are welcome to flick to the end of the book to check it out.

For Sheppard

*Your music is epic. I love your sound and your style.
Thank you for inspiring this story with your music.*

And

For Ed Sheeran

*Thank you for writing the most beautiful love song
I've ever heard. You are one of the most talented
musicians out there and you inspire me.*

ONE

JANE

The summer breeze tickled my skin as I stood outside the small stone chapel. White cloud puffs floated like cruising ships in the blue sky while the sun beat down on my pale skin. I'd have to move soon or risk getting burned. My large, floppy hat protected my freckled face but my arms were exposed.

Rubbing my hands over them, I inched closer to my personal nightmare.

I thought coming back to the place it all ended would bring me some kind of comfort, but all I felt was despair. It had been just over a year since my best friend, Sarah, and I giggled our way up the stone path, my wedding dress draped across my arm. Giddy excitement had made us dance and act like schoolgirls. I was getting married. It was meant to be the most thrilling day of my life. And it was...until my mother opened the door to the dressing room.

"He's gone, love." Her eyes were messy with tears, her skin pale.

"What do you mean?" I gripped the bench seat I was sitting on, not wanting to match the words with her expression. It couldn't be true. Blake wouldn't leave me on our wedding day. We loved each other.

He was my soul mate.

My everything.

"Justin and his father are heading to the crash site now."

My heart went limp. It deflated to a flat pancake and slithered into my belly while a thick, pounding beat pulsed through my head.

Sarah gripped my shoulder, her voice coming out broken and wispy. "How?"

"Motorcycle accident." Mum's voice turned to white noise, the throbbing inside me drowning out anything other than one simple fact: the love of my life was dead and he wouldn't be marrying me.

Not that day.

Not ever.

Tears burned my eyes as I gritted my teeth and glared at the wooden doors, the ones Blake and I were supposed to run through while people blew bubbles over our heads.

Sarah and I had planned the day to perfection.

The perfect wedding to start the perfect life.

Instead it had become my worst nightmare. One I couldn't seem to recover from.

Turning my back on the chapel, I headed to my rental car. Mum told me I could have just borrowed one from Aunt Helen, but I didn't want the family knowing I was there. She seemed to understand my reasoning. My return to England was not a catch-up.

I was looking for...

What? I still wasn't sure.

I had to move on.

I figured out about a month ago that no matter how hard I wished for it, I was still waking up every morning, alive and well. It hit me like a mallet to the face that I could be doing that for the next seventy-five years. Was I really prepared to keep trudging away at life, acting like a robot so I didn't have to feel Blake's loss so deeply?

I couldn't do it.

I had to find my way, figure out how to be a person without him.

Dumping my hat on the passenger seat, I started the car and pulled away from the church, heading back toward Rye. It was the cutest, most adorable town in southern England. Only a few miles from the ocean, with quaint, cobbled streets and pubs that were hundreds of years old. My mother had lived there for a short time as a child, and when I came to visit the summer before I started college, I fell in love with it. When she showed me the church she and Dad had gotten married in, I was determined to keep that tradition going. I didn't know at the time that I'd meet *the one* only a month after thinking that…and I definitely had no idea I'd be burying him in New Mexico five years later.

A bitter scoff punched out of my mouth and I gripped the wheel. I was nearing the corner.

The dreaded corner.

My parents wouldn't let me go to the crash site in my wedding dress. I was firing for the door when Dad stopped me, wrapping his arms around me and whimpering. "You won't want to see. Please, baby, don't remember him that way."

In retrospect, I guess they were right. I'd never had the heart to truly investigate the accident. I didn't know the other driver in the collision. Some woman who was speeding through the countryside, unprepared to find Blake on the wrong side of the road.

If I ever felt particularly weak-minded, I'd let myself imagine the crash.

Slowing the car, I pulled to the edge of the road and stared at the corner, picturing Blake on his bike. He'd always been so sexy on his bike. I'd never forget the first time I saw him, pulling up to the curb and taking off his helmet before catching my eye and grinning at me. His wild shoulder-length curls, that cocky glint in his eyes. It'd taken me all of a week to fall in love with him.

I sniffed and flinched as I saw the crash in my

mind, heard the crunch of metal, watched Blake's body fly through the air and land with a sickening thud in the ditch. Apparently he smashed his head on a rock. It indented his skull, making him unrecognizable.

Gripping my mouth, I closed my eyes against the burning sting of tears and turned away from the empty road. I wanted to hate him for not wearing a helmet, but I couldn't. Instead I cursed the female driver for not obeying the speed limit, for not having enough time to brake and swerve away from my American sweetheart on the wrong side of the road.

Why couldn't road rules be universal?

I slapped the wheel and then drove on, checking the road twice to ensure I was adhering to British law. The wheel was on the other side of the car, which helped. Blake had been on a bike though. He wouldn't have had that same reminder.

He'd told me he had a surprise planned for right after the ceremony.

When I'd kissed him good night the evening before, he'd whispered in my ear. "I'm stealing you away before the reception, beautiful. Can't be sharing our first married moment with a big crowd, now can we?"

The romantic smile on his face had made my heart swell so big I thought it'd burst.

Reaching Rye, I continued through the small village, heading out to the rolling hills on the other side. The cliffs were drawing near and I kept going, wondering what I'd find when I reached the isolated spot.

I couldn't help wondering if this was where Blake had intended to whisk me off to...on the bike he'd secretly hired. My wedding dress would have been billowing behind the back wheel. I would have clung to him, no doubt worrying about dirtying the cream-colored tulle. Blake would have just smiled and told me to relax.

"Enjoy the moment, carrots."

The only person on earth I ever let call me a nickname related to my hair. Funny how much I missed it.

A sad smile wafted over my lips as I exited the car and trudged up the hill. The wind picked up as I crested the rise, sweeping the hair off my face and making me feel like I was in some shampoo commercial. Planting my feet at the top of the cliff, I looked out across the vast ocean, so blue and icy cold. Inching to the very edge, I gazed down and wondered what it'd feel like to jump. To throw myself into the abyss and fly for a few glorious moments before crashing to my death.

Death.

I'd thought about it almost every day since Blake left me, but I could never bring myself to do it. As much as I wanted all the pain to end, my survival instincts wouldn't let me take my life. I had to keep going somehow.

Stepping back from the edge, I walked through the vibrant green grass, spotting a small group of tourists below me. My forehead wrinkled and I spun away from them, heading further up the hill until I reached a lone tree.

Placing my hand on the bark, I ran my fingers over the rough surface.

"Well, you look like you've survived okay all by yourself." I looked up to the thick branches, appreciating the way the light and leaves cast shadows together, giving the tree depth and beauty. "I don't suppose you care to tell me how you've done it."

The leaves rustled and swayed in response.

I sighed and walked around the trunk, the pads of my fingers dancing over the bark until I reached the other side. Jerking to a stop, I pulled in a sharp breath, my eyes flooding with tears as I traced the letters carved into the wood.

Jane + Blake
1000 years

The words were framed by a heart.

I managed a shaky laugh, my face bunching as tears slid from my eyes.

"Our song," I whispered.

"A Thousand Years." It was supposed to play as I walked down the aisle toward him. Instead it played as his coffin was carried out of his family church in Albuquerque.

Pressing two fingers against my lips, I kissed them, then placed that kiss on the trunk.

"I'll love you for a thousand years, baby. And a thousand more."

My body started to tremble. I could picture him

so clearly. He would have looked so handsome in his chocolate brown wedding suit, his hair tied back in a stubby ponytail. He would have brushed my lower lip with his thumb and kissed me under that tree—our first moment together as a married couple.

I dropped to my knees, the tree roots scraping my skin as I covered my mouth and cried. I missed him so much. Every day was a chore without him. Every lonely minute so depleting.

Sucking in a ragged breath, I let out another sob and forced my mind back to our wedding day. He must have ridden up to the tree that morning to carve his sweet message before heading to the chapel.

Slapping my hand on the trunk, I dug my fingers into the bark, trying to absorb Blake's last moment. To somehow make it mine. His feet would have been planted where my knees sat, his pocketknife blade digging into the wood as he no doubt smiled and thought of me.

I wanted to stay in that beautiful moment with him, to leave a part of myself behind so our souls could endure together.

My eyes flicked to the emerald on my wedding finger. I still hadn't found the courage to remove the engagement ring Blake gave me, but for reasons I didn't understand, I wriggled it off my finger. With quick, erratic breaths, I gouged my nails into the dry soil between the roots until I'd created a big enough hole to place the ring inside.

Kissing the sparkly green stone, I dropped it

into my hiding place before I could change my mind. I took my time covering it up, muttering prayers that it would never be found. The longer I worked, the more convinced I was that leaving my ring at the base of the tree would somehow combine Blake and me for life.

I'd never love again, I was certain of it. My heart was too full with Blake to let another in. The whole reason I came back to the beginning was to figure out how to live alone—how to start my life anew. Leaving my ring with Blake, making this spot ours, was a step in the right direction.

Satisfied the ring was now a part of the precious tree, I stood back and wrapped my arms around myself. Gazing at the carved words, I stood in my spot, whisper-singing our song from beginning to end.

"I'm yours forever, Blake." I brushed the pads of my fingers over his carving. "I love you."

Turning from our tree, I ambled back to the car, my soul flirting with that peace I'd been so desperately craving. It wasn't all-consuming, just the whisper of hope that somehow I could do this. I could move on. I could keep going. I *would* find my way.

Happiness didn't need to be out of my grasp anymore.

Blake was still with me. We were joined for life.

It was time for me to start living again…for the both of us.

TWO

HARRY

I wasn't actually in the mood for drinking, but it was Wednesday night and I always went to the pub on Wednesdays. Devan and her brother, Tommy, tended bar mid-week, and they were often good for a laugh. I needed a laugh that night. Work had been hard going, with one annoying client who just couldn't seem to believe I had a better eye for design than he did. It was only my full-time job, right? What the hell would I know about marketing and enticing people to stay on a website? Like a busy, over-cluttered home page would get people clicking. It didn't help that he owned the world's smallest bookstore and was somehow under the delusion that a website would make it world-famous.

I cringed, looking forward to wrapping up with him as soon as possible. Pulling the door wide, the music hit me immediately. The thump of the drum and strum of the guitar filled me with the sense of calm it always did. People's chatter added to the hum of noise coming from the friendly pub. There was a familiarity about the place that comforted me every time. I stepped aside to make way for Mr. and Mrs. Fedley, nodding and saying hello to the middle-aged couple. They'd been coming to The Whistle Inn since I was a baby in a high chair. I'd been born and raised in the little town of Rye. Sure, I'd spread my wings to London, and Europe for holidays, but I always seemed to find my way back home. I told myself it was because of Nan. She was eighty-nine and not exactly getting younger, but some days I wondered if I was just a big, fat liar.

I'd been itching to go overseas for months, and that itch just kept getting stronger. I knew escape wouldn't save me from what happened, but it'd been a while now and maybe I was ready to move on.

With a sniff, I pushed my hands into my pockets and sauntered up to the bar, ready to take my usual seat and order a pint of Guinness.

But something stopped me.

Something red and intriguing.

A girl I'd never seen in the Whistle before.

We got a lot of tourists in Rye. I wasn't

complaining; it kept my mum's B&B afloat. I usually didn't pay them much attention. But they weren't usually pretty little redheads with pale skin, ginger freckles, and eyes as green as emeralds. They weren't usually sitting all by themselves with sad smiles on their pink lips. The end of a pen was nipped between her teeth as she gazed down at a crumpled sheet of paper.

I rested my hand on the bar, unable to stop myself from stealing another glimpse of her. Why was she so sad? Something about her face seemed to radiate a heartbreaking loneliness.

I understood it.

My heart squeezed and writhed within me, urging me to turn away from the girl...and my memories.

But I couldn't.

"Pint of Guinny, Harry?" Devan asked.

"Yeah." I nodded, keeping my eyes on the stranger. She was taking a sip of beer. The glass mug looked huge in her slender hands. Her fingers were long. Everything about her seemed long and elegant. Her hands were more suited to a wineglass than a tankard of ale.

Devan slapped a cardboard coaster by my elbow, followed by the pint. I curled my fingers around the handle and took a slow sip.

"If you keep staring at her like that she's going to think you're a serial killer."

I swiveled on my stool and grinned at my friend. She was a few years older than me but we went to school together. She used to bully me on the playground until my older brother, Simon, punched her one. Still couldn't believe he hit a girl, but Simon argued that she'd been hitting me for years and it was only fair. Enough was enough.

And it was.

Battle ended. Friendship begun.

"Do you know anything about her?" I brushed the curls off my forehead.

Devan looked at me in surprise, resting her hands against the bar and smirking. "You really interested in this girl?"

"No." I scoffed. "I just..." Looking over my shoulder, I took in her sad loneliness and sensed the commonality between us.

Her green eyes darted toward me as if she could sense my gaze. I offered a closed-mouth smile which she returned before glancing at the stage.

O'Brian's was playing. They were my favorite local band, always choosing the perfect covers. Nothing too loud or obnoxious, just brilliant background music to set the right tone. They must have been on a Sheppard kick that week, because they started playing "Be More Barrio," and I was positive I'd heard it at least twice every time they performed.

Devan confirmed my thinking with an eye roll. "Here we go. Set number two, exactly the same as last night."

"It's not so bad." I lifted my chin at the stage. "I like this song."

"You're not the only one." Devan tipped her head toward the round table to my right, and I glanced at the redhead again.

She was bobbing her head in time to the beat, a soft smile pulling at her lips.

"Do you know anything?" I took another sip of beer, wondering why I was so curious. It wasn't like I wanted to get involved with another girl. I'd learned from experience that love could rip your heart out. I'd only just gotten it back inside my chest; I wasn't about to risk losing it all over again.

I turned away, reminding myself not to be a fool.

"All I know is that she came in here yesterday and booked a room for two nights. She sounds American to me."

"Right." I nodded then shook my head, hunching over the bar and resisting the urge to approach her.

I didn't even understand it. I wasn't interested!

Inevitably, my gaze traveled back, drawn by her red hair...or maybe the distant, familiar look in her eyes. She nibbled her bottom lip, then took a breath and crossed something off on her sheet of paper. Blinking rapidly, she stared at the sheet, the paper trembling ever so slightly in her hands.

"Go on." Devan flicked my shoulder. "Show some courage, man. There's no harm in talking to her."

"Be More Barrio" finished, and like some kind of sign from the gods, the guitarist started in with the familiar riff of "Geronimo." I knew the song before the lead singer had even opened his mouth. It had become a favorite of mine.

Spinning on my stool, I gulped down the rest of my beer and slapped the mug on the counter. Wiping my mouth with the back of my hand, I straightened my shirt, whispered "Geronimo," and walked toward the lonely redhead and her mysterious sheet of paper.

THREE

JANE

I sensed him approaching and turned as he closed the distance. I had no idea who he was or why he wanted to talk to me.

I mean, I guess I had some vague idea. But I'd been out of the dating scene for a very long time. In fact, I'd met Blake in my first couple of weeks at Stanford, so I kind of felt like I'd never really been *in* the dating scene.

I wasn't interested of course, but I didn't want to be rude, so when the scruffy-haired, unshaven guy stopped by my table and gave me a kind smile, I reciprocated.

My lips felt stiff and awkward, and I looked back to the stage the second after our eyes met.

"Hi, um…" He raised his hand in greeting. "Hi."

"Hello," I clipped then bit my lips together, keeping my head away from him but aware of everything out of the corner of my eye—the long dimples that formed on his cheeks when he grinned, the way his sharp nose twitched as his eyes darted to the rumpled piece of paper on the table. Sliding the list into my hand, I folded it and tucked it away in my back pocket.

"I hope you don't mind me just coming up to you like this. I'm not interested in trying to woo you or get you to have sex with me. Don't get me wrong, you're very attractive. I'm just… I'm not interested…in that. I mean, I like sex, very much, but I'm not standing here with some classy one-liner up my sleeve and a bunch of ulterior motives. I just wanted to make that clear before I introduced myself. Although, after this completely absurd first impression, I'm guessing you'll be kicking me back to the bar any moment now."

Oh man, he was adorable.

His accent combined with the nervous drivel coming out of his mouth… I couldn't help a little snort and snicker. I slapped my hand over my mouth and nose, my shoulders shaking as I tried to contain my laughter.

The guy winced and pinched the bridge of his nose. "Do you mind if I start again?"

"By all means." I giggled.

"Okay." He nodded and then puffed out a breath, sticking out his hand and saying, "Hi, my name's Harry Tindal. I live here in the lovely town of Rye, and I would just like to welcome you."

I wrapped my fingers around his hand, noticing the quiet strength behind his grasp. "Hello, Harry. I'm Georjana Buford."

I have no idea what possessed me to use my full name. My mother was about the only person on the planet to ever refer to me as Georjana. I inwardly cringed, waiting for that standard look of pity.

But Harry just grinned. "Ah, like the duchess."

I raised my eyebrows and nodded. "Almost. Slightly different spelling, but I think my mother had Georgiana Cavendish in mind when she named me. Not only does she teach history, but she's a sucker for those royals." I took a sip of my beer, liking the taste of it, hoping it'd numb the nerves bouncing around inside of me. I was talking to a strange man in a pub. I didn't do that kind of thing.

I licked my top lip, trying to decide if I should invite him to sit down or not.

He was standing there, waiting for me, so I cleared my throat and smiled. "She'll always be a proud patriot, I guess."

Harry's eyes narrowed and he took a seat anyway, balancing his long body on the edge of the stool beside me. "You know, for a Brit, you have quite the American accent."

I chuckled. "My father's American, and he met my mother when he moved here to start working at the American Embassy. I actually lived in London until I was fifteen."

"Yet you lost your accent?"

"I'm sure it will return soon enough. It often does when I'm back here."

He smiled at me again, his gaze warm. His eyes were hazel—could have been brown or green depending on the light. There was a soft sparkle in them. It reminded me of Sarah. Some people just oozed kindness...and Harry was one of them.

Comforted by my conclusion, I leaned my arms on the table, lightly threading my fingers together, aware of the missing ring on my fourth finger. It was nearly enough to send me running for my room, but something kept me grounded, gave me the courage to smile and ask, "So, Harry, what brings you to my table this evening?"

"Oh! Uh, Dutch courage?" He chuckled and shook his head. "Actually, I don't know. I just saw you sitting over here and you looked lonely and then the song started playing and well..." He shrugged. "Geronimo, I suppose."

"Geronimo." I snickered, glancing at the stage. The song was coming to an end, the female backup singing, "Bombs away." I bobbed my head and smiled.

"So, uh, Georjana, what brings you to the little town of Rye?"

"Jane." My heart thrummed a wild beat as I tried to avoid the question. "Just Jane."

"Okay." He grinned. "So, what brings you to my town, Just Jane?"

I laughed at his quip, scratching my chin and being as vague as I could. "Self-discovery, I guess."

"Oh, really." He leaned in to the table. "Well, that is intriguing."

The way his hazel eyes searched my face made me pull back. Leaning away from him, I forgot there was no back to my stool and started to wobble. He captured my arm, steadying me while I let out a breathy, embarrassed chuckle.

"You all right?" He patted my elbow then let me go.

I could still feel his fingers on me though. It made me realize how long it'd been since I'd been touched by a man.

"Yes, I'm fine. I'm just…" I cleared my throat and ran my finger beneath my long bangs, tucking them behind my right ear.

"You're not drunk already, are you? It's only eight o'clock."

I laughed and shook my head, my skin no doubt glowing red. I hated my pale white skin and giveaway blush.

Tapping the table, Harry turned and waved his finger at the bartender. She nodded and called, "I'll bring you one in a sec, love."

Turning back with a friendly smile, he bumped my arm with his knuckle. "Tell me, how do you plan on discovering yourself? Is there a magic formula no one's told me about?"

"No. I wish." I cringed and ran my finger round the lip of my mug. "I have two weeks before I need to get back for work, and I thought I'd come over here and see where the road takes me. Try to cross a few things off my list."

"Hang on." He frowned at me. "You're going to see where the road takes you, but you've made a list? Isn't that a contradiction?"

"It's not that kind of list." I hesitated, wondering why I was compelled to show him. The only other person who'd seen it was Sarah.

His hazel eyes studied me, the warm smile within them enough to have me reaching for my back pocket. My cheeks were already burning red; I figured I may as well make them neon.

Unfolding the sheet of paper, I cleared my throat and placed my list on the table between us.

"Jane's Life List," Harry murmured, picking it up and scanning the contents. I had about ten things on there. A mix of the simple, like reading *The Great Gatsby* and watching *Gone with the Wind*, to the adventurous, like skydiving and learning how to surf.

His lips curled at the edges, and I guessed he was up to the two Sarah added before I left on my trip: horseback riding on the beach and skinny-dipping in the ocean.

"Nice." He nodded and then passed it back to me. "Aren't those normally called a bucket list?"

"Yes, well." I tipped my head, gazing at my scribble. "I decided to change the title."

"Why?" He asked it so softly, so nicely, I started answering him before even thinking about it.

"I've been in a rut, I guess you could say, and I just needed something to bring me back to life."

I hoped it was a sufficient answer. I really didn't want to go into detail.

Harry went still, studying me with a look of wonder. My words obviously resonated with him, because a slow smile worked over his lips and he started nodding.

"I like the sound of that," he whispered.

Our eyes connected, pulled together by something we shared. I wasn't sure what it was but I sensed an understanding. Forcing my gaze away, I concentrated on refolding my list and putting it back in my pocket.

"So, that first item you crossed off. The 'saying goodbye' one. Is that some metaphor for leaving your rut behind?"

I wasn't about to tell him the truth, that I crossed it off because today at my tree, I realized that Blake would always be with me. I didn't need to say goodbye to him anymore. We were destined to spend eternity together, and I could go forward and achieve the list for both of us.

But for some reason, I didn't want to bring Blake into my conversation with Harry, so instead I just smiled and mumbled, "Something like that."

"Well, you're in the perfect place to do some of those things. Europe's just a stone's throw away. I can already think of about three different places you could go to start crossing off your list...and adding to it." He winked.

His reaction inspired me and I pulled out the list again, smoothing it out on the table and uncapping the pen with my teeth. Blake danced through my mind, powering ideas through my head. A smile worked over my lips as I imagined him beside me, coaxing the truth out of me.

"Come on, carrots, what are we going to do? Be wild about it, honey. Make me proud."

I chuckled and started writing and talking at the same time. "I want to see something ancient and beautiful. I want to soak in the sun. Swim in water so clear I can see my toes." I looked down at what I'd added.

See an ancient wonder.

Swim in crystal clear waters.

Tapping my pen on the sheet of paper, I glanced up at Harry and kept going. "I just want to stop thinking and get outside of my own head. I want to *live* and do things that will make me laugh. I want to feel unchecked joy. I want to be crazy and spontaneous." I could hear Blake's voice in my words.

Harry's awe-filled gaze was still in place, his eyes searching my expression.

Would he think I was a fraud? I was sitting there spouting stuff that would have come from Blake's mouth. But as I said them, I realized how badly I wanted that dream honeymoon Blake and I had planned. He'd been set on making me do a bunch of crazy stuff, pulling me out of my comfort zone. I had a responsibility to do it, didn't I?

Suddenly stunted by doubts, I looked back at my list.

Would I have the courage to go through with any of them?

Recapping my pen, I laid it down on the paper and frowned. My shoulders slumped as I leaned my elbows on the table. "I'm probably coming across like some crazy person. I don't even know if I can do these things. I'm not wild. I plan, I organize. I like to know exactly what's going on, so why the hell do I think I can do this?"

Because Blake would have wanted me to.

Harry distracted me with his soft voice. "I don't think you're crazy. You're coming across like a woman who's in search of a new future. There's nothing wrong with that."

I gave him a grateful smile, glad when he was distracted by the lady bringing him a beer.

"Thanks, darling."

She smiled and slapped his shoulder, winking at me before turning back to the bar.

Lifting his mug, Harry tipped it at me then took a sip.

The crowd cheered as the band brought their next song to an end. "Thanks so much. We've got time for one more song. Any requests?"

I smiled and shouted, "Geronimo," at exactly the same time as Harry.

Our heads snapped to look at each other, and we both pointed and said, "Jinx!" Again, at the exact same time, then laughed.

I didn't know what it was about the guy, but it was very easy being with him, chatting with him like we'd known each other for years. Laughing together as the band started up "Geronimo" one more time.

I clapped my hands and cheered, grinning at Harry, who had stopped watching the band and was staring at me with this intense sparkle in his eyes. Before I could figure it out, he leaned forward and shocked the hell out of me.

"I want to help you cross some of these things off your list."

My eyes narrowed with caution.

"Hear me out..." He rubbed his hands together. "You're after two weeks of sun, fun, and adventure. I could use the same thing. Why don't we go together? We'll just hit the road tomorrow morning and try to cross off as many of these as we can." He tapped the sheet of paper.

My eyes bulged, ready to fall right out of my head. I should have been tipping my head back in laughter and telling him to get lost. As if I would go off with some stranger on a two-week road trip. That was insanity plus!

But...

He laughed at my expression. "I know it's crazy."

It was! Still lost for words, I tried to figure out why I wasn't saying no.

"But you can trust me, okay? I'm seriously a good guy. And if it makes you feel better, we can put some rules around it." He started counting on his fingers. "No sex. No histories. No awkward conversations. Just two people living life to the max for two weeks. Then we say adios, thanks for a good time, and go our separate ways. You'd get that self-discovery you're looking for, and not only would I get a much-needed break, but I'd have the satisfaction of knowing I helped you on your quest." His smile was so hopeful and expectant...so hard to resist.

"So, say Geronimo! Say Geronimo!" the singers shouted into the microphones, encouraging the crowd to join in.

I gazed across the pub, the beat of the music thumping through me, Harry's proposal drumming in my brain. I wanted to say yes. That was what I couldn't understand.

But it was the only answer on my mind.

A. Big. Fat. Yes.

"So, what do you say, Jane?" Harry called above the crowd.

I bit my lips together, my brain screaming at me to use some common sense. I couldn't say yes. That was crazy. Glancing across at Harry, I took in his expectant, hopeful face, the kindness in his eyes, and blurted, "Geronimo?"

"Geronimo?" The sparkles in his eyes seemed to dance. "As in yes?"

My head bobbed of its own accord. "Geronimo," I repeated.

Clapping his hands together, he let out a loud laugh, then slapped the table. "Geronimo!"

I raised my mug and shouted, "Geronimo!"

Joining me, he raised his own mug and held it close to mine. "To craziness."

"To songs that make us brave."

"To Dutch courage." He tapped his glass against mine, and with excited, kid-like smiles we toasted his completely insane idea.

FOUR

HARRY

Working my jaw to the side, I pulled Nan's car up to The Whistle Inn and hopped out. My head was just a little achy from my Dutch courage, but it would clear soon enough. I sipped at the coffee Nan had painstakingly made for me. I tried to tell her not to but she wouldn't have it.

"Let me do this for you, love." Her warning look reminded me that she was in fact my elder, and I backed off, patiently waiting while she prepared two coffees with her shaky hands. I subtly texted Mum one more time to double-check someone would be popping in on Nan at lunchtime. Part of me felt guilty for leaving the fragile woman, but when I told her about the trip, her eyes brimmed with pride and she offered to help me pack.

I checked that the thermos mug for Jane was still sitting upright in the passenger's seat before leaning against the yellow car door and crossing my ankles.

The gentlemanly thing to do would have been to escort Jane out of the hotel. But I didn't want Jane thinking I was pushing the boundaries of our deal. I was determined to stick with the rules I'd listed, for both our sakes.

I hadn't had sex since my mindless bout of "get over Tammy" one-night stands. It wasn't until I woke up beside a girl I couldn't stand that I realized I was being a complete tosser about the whole thing. Humping anything with tits would not mend my broken heart, and sleeping with Jane wouldn't either.

When she'd said that she was trying to bring herself back to life, it struck a chord with me. I needed the same thing. I was ashamed by just how long my rut had lasted. At first I'd filled it up with booze, then sex. Once I realized they were set on destroying me, I turned to work and caring for my nan. Although they were both good things to devote myself to, they hadn't eased the itch, the nagging sensation that I needed more.

My sister suggested a few weeks ago, when I was struggling through a restless day, that it was probably time I thought about falling in love again. But that was complete bullocks. I wasn't willing to risk my heart for a woman again.

Sliding my shades up, I squinted at the inn doors as one opened to reveal a shock of red hair. Jane had a large backpack slung over her shoulder and a set of keys in her hands. Her long, pale legs were on display, her olive green dress catching on the breeze as she shut the door behind her. I caught a flash of white knickers before she slapped her hand over the material with a little "Oh!"

I grinned, having to admit that the view wasn't bad.

Glancing across the street, she stopped short and then gaped at me...and my little Bambino. Her eyes narrowed as she cautiously walked toward us.

"What is that?" She pointed at the car I was leaning against.

I gave her a proud smile and turned to run my hand over the roof of the midget vehicle. "This is my nan's Bambino."

Her skeptical frown was comical. "Is it supposed to be a car? Because I've actually rented a grown-up one, and I seriously think we should take it. It has four doors and doesn't look like it was bought at a toy store."

I chuckled. "Now, now, be nice to the car. She's served my nan very well, and she's plenty strong enough to take us to Europe."

"But..." Jane pulled a dubious face, her forehead wrinkling.

"Come on, Jane. Do you honestly want to tell your friends back home that you took a two-week road trip in a boring old rental car? Think about it.

You could be telling them that you experienced life to the max in a gorgeous yellow Bambino!" I spread my arms, highlighting the car and putting on my secondhand car dealer's face.

Jane stared at me for a long beat, then snorted out a laugh. "This is insane."

"Well, you said you wanted to be crazy. I'm just here to help."

Pursing her lips, she looked down the road at what I assumed was her rental car and then back to Yambi—Nan's name, not mine.

"Will the rental car be okay here for two weeks?"

"Yeah, I'll just call and let Devan know not to tow it."

I pulled out my phone and texted my friend, resisting the urge to run around and open Jane's door. It went against everything I'd been taught, but I wasn't there to woo the girl. I was just there to help her cross off that list.

Our doors slammed in unison once we were settled into the car. Jane sipped her coffee and let out a satisfied moan.

"Oh, I so needed this. Thank you."

I started the car. "My nan's the world's best cook...and coffee maker." I swallowed back the urge to admit that she also had Parkinson's and her cooking days were basically over. It hurt to even think it.

"You're obviously close to her."

"Yeah." I nodded, doing a U-turn and heading east out of Rye. "My grandfather died about ten years ago and then…" I swallowed, not wanting to go into it, grateful for my no-histories clause in our arrangement. "I moved in with her about six months ago, just to help her out."

Jane accepted my answer with a smile. "That's nice of you."

"Well, she's pretty cool for an old bird." I winked, enjoying the sound of her laughter.

We drove in silence for about ten minutes, Jane distracted by the view. Funny how it sometimes takes a visitor to make you realize how beautiful your own country is.

I got lost in the rolling hills and summer sunshine until Jane turned to me and asked, "So, where are we going?"

"Well, like I said last night, Europe's a good start, so we're heading to the Chunnel right now, and we'll catch the train to Coquelles."

"Wow," Jane murmured.

That word and her awed expression reminded me that I'd made the right call. I'd slaved over my laptop until three a.m., preparing everything so I could take a couple of weeks off. I could actually work from anywhere, so I brought my laptop to finish up a few things while Jane was… I don't know…reading *The Great Gatsby*.

"Which reminds me," I blurted, forgetting I hadn't been thinking aloud. Reaching behind me, I wrestled with the zipper of my pack, keeping an eye on the road and tugging out a copy of the book.

My throat grew thick with emotion as I glanced at the worn cover, remembering the petite hands that used to hold it, devouring the book while she curled up in bed on a rainy weekend morning.

I missed those days.

Dropping the book into Jane's lap, I forced a grin. "There you go, love."

She picked up the novel and gave me a delighted gasp, running her hand over the cover and trying to flatten out the curled corners.

"It's not for keeps, I just thought you might like to borrow it, so… you know, don't drop it in the ocean when you're skinny-dipping."

Jane laughed, whacking my arm lightly with the book. "I'll do no such thing." Glancing down at the cover, she shook her head and smiled at me. "Can't believe you remembered."

"It was only last night." I chuckled. "And I told you, I'm here to help you cross off that list."

"Well, we're off to a pretty good start." She nestled back in her seat, curling her fingers around the book on her lap and sipping at her coffee.

Switching on the little portable speaker on the dash, I then connected my phone and pressed play. "Best Day of My Life" kicked in, and we both grinned then started singing along. She knew the lyrics as well as I did, and it wasn't hard to conclude that this could be one of the best holidays I'd ever had.

*****

Nine hours later we were driving through the streets of Paris. I'd been there a few times before and sort of knew my way around. I was heading for a small boutique hotel, the owner an acquaintance of my mum's through the hospitality business. They didn't know each other that well, but I figured a little name-dropping might score me a special room rate.

Jane stared out the window, blinking slowly at the view. She'd gone quiet about an hour ago. I guess after eight hours of talking and singing she was pretty tired.

I was.

But I was also happy...and I hadn't felt that kind of comfortable joy in a long time.

I relished it as I navigated through the narrow streets and slowly found my way to Rue Christine. It was an old, quiet street near the Latin Quarter. Black street lamps that reminded me of Narnian fairytales lined the straight lane, highlighting the row of arched doorways.

"We're nearly here," I murmured.

Turning onto the road, I was grateful for Nan's little Bambino. It was so much easier to navigate in the big cities.

"Ah, here we go." I stopped and pointed to the quaint hotel.

Jane's face lit with an instant smile as she drank it in. "It's gorgeous."

The small cobblestone courtyard was guarded by a wrought iron gate and made beautiful with splashes of green vines draping from the upper balconies. In the early evening light, the hotel looked nothing less than enchanting.

"I can't believe I'm actually doing this."

I grinned at her awed whisper, then leaned across and murmured, "And this is only the beginning."

She turned to smile at me, her green eyes doing something to my insides that I hadn't felt in a long time. I shied away from it, looking back at the road and concentrating on finding a place to park.

Fifteen minutes later, we were checking in. The owner remembered my mother and set us up in separate rooms, I on the first floor and Jane on the second.

"*Bienvenue à Paris. La ville de l'amour.*" The owner's eyes sparkled.

I chuckled, sliding the keys into my pocket and shaking my head. "*Mon amie et moi sommes seulement ici pour la nourriture et le vin.*"

She laughed and flicked her hand at me, like she knew better and I was a dumb fool to think I could stay in this city with such a pretty girl and not fall in love with her.

As we walked to the elevator, Jane tugged on my sleeve and whispered, "I haven't spoken French since I was fifteen. What did you just say?"

"She was joking that Paris is the city of love, and I told her you and I are simply here for the food and wine."

Jane smiled, looking relieved by my answer. We stepped into the elevator, and I pressed the one then the two. "Well, if that's what we're here for, I guess we better get out there and enjoy it."

"Sounds like a plan to me. How long does it take

a girl like you to get ready?"

The elevator dinged and I stepped out, once again having to resist the urge to walk her to her room. I'd never been such an un-gentleman in my life. My mother would have been horrified.

Jane's green eyes twinkled. "Give me thirty minutes."

"I'll meet you in the lobby."

And I did.

My hair was still wet from my shower, but at least I smelled fresh. Jane arrived about a minute after I did, and we walked into the evening air together. It was only seven o'clock but felt more like nine. All that driving, as pleasant as it was, exhausted me. I was looking forward to a good meal, some fine wine, and a decent sleep.

I had to admit, it was nice being with a girl and having zero expectations. Laying down those rules had taken all the awkwardness out of this weird setup, and we strolled down the street like longtime friends.

I didn't know much about her history. She'd told me a couple of anecdotes from her childhood as we drove to Paris, but we mostly kept our getting-to-know-each-other info to the present-day. Suited me just fine; I wasn't about to ruin everything by opening up about my heartache.

Jane taught twelve- and thirteen-year-olds at a private middle school. She didn't tell me where, and I didn't ask.

I was determined not to probe too deep. I didn't want to know. Light and fun was the only way to do it.

"What's your room like?" Jane's eyes danced with humor. "Mine's insane. The wallpaper is like an acid trip, and it's in the same fabric as the duvet cover. I just stood in my doorway for like five minutes feeling dizzy." She laughed. "It's so fantastic!"

I grinned and nodded. "Mine's green and white with this cool King Louis vibe."

Jane leaned against me and laughed. "I still can't believe I'm doing this! When I came over here, I honestly had no idea how I was going to get through my list."

"Why did you choose to start in Rye? It's hardly the extreme adventure capital of the world."

Jane bit her lips together, her head stiff as she shook it.

"Ah." I nodded. "Not a problem. We don't have to talk about anything you don't want to." I nudged her arm with my elbow. "This trip is about the here and now. No awkward conversations allowed."

Her smile grew, her stiff posture giving way to a relaxed sigh.

"This way." I pointed down the street and directed her to the restaurant the lady at the hotel had recommended to us.

They sat us at a tiny table in the back. It was crowded with French chatter and smells so good my mouth started salivating.

"*Merci*." I took the menu from the waiter and scanned the text. "Do you need help reading anything?"

Jane pursed her lips, her eyebrows dipping into a V as she tried to decipher the menu. After a moment, she put it down with a huff. "I can't believe how much I've forgotten. I took French for three years at school. Why are you so good at it?"

"Because my mother was a homework Nazi. She was determined that we aced whatever we did. My sister, Renee, and I were both taking French, and she used to have these enforced 'French' days where we were only allowed to speak to each other in French." I rolled my eyes. "Bloody painful."

Jane leaned across the table and grinned. "Yeah, but I bet you're bloody grateful now, right?"

I smiled at her. "Okay, so my little French illiterate, what do you want to eat?"

"I'm not sure what I feel like." She picked up the menu again.

"Well, what's your favorite type of food?"

"Chocolate mousse." She bit at her smile, her cheeks flooding with color.

Oh man, that skin could go red in a heartbeat.

Adorable.

I cleared my throat, trying to ward off that familiar wave of affection. I'd only ever felt it for Tammy, and I wasn't about to fall into that trap again.

"Well, *mousse au chocolat* is on here, along with, oh..." I licked my lips. "Clafoutis, crème brûlée, chouquettes, lemon tart," I groaned. "This is the best dessert menu in the world."

Jane licked her bottom lip, making it glisten.

"They all sound so good. How do we decide?"

"We don't." I shrugged. "We simply order them all."

Her pale eyebrows popped high. "Are you serious right now?"

"Why not?" I laughed. "This trip is about being crazy and spontaneous. Who needs meat and vegetables when you can pig out on sugar and deliciousness."

"We'll feel so sick afterwards."

I rested my elbows on the table until my face hovered above the candle. "But it'll be so worth it."

Her face lit with the kind of smile a guy could fall for. I probably should have leaned away from it, but I couldn't. I just soaked it in until the waiter appeared and I ordered the most insane dinner of my life.

The waiter frowned and then looked to Jane, who just bobbed her head with a cheeky grin.

"*D'accord*." He nodded, taking our menus and shaking his head. "*Est-ce que vous désirez boire du vin avec votre repas?*"

I looked to Jane. "Wine?"

Her nose wrinkled. "We might have to stick with water or risk falling into sugar-induced comas."

"Good plan." I nodded and told the waiter, but he'd already heard her and was quietly laughing.

As he walked away to fulfill our order, I shifted back in my seat and stared across the table at my travel partner, more and more sure that this would be one of the best holidays I'd ever had.

I'd spent too many years letting life pass me by, taking for granted the things I'd had before me. My relaxed attitude had lost me everything, and I wasn't going to make the same mistake twice. Life was about living in the moment, and Jane's quest would force me to become the man I should have been two years ago when Tammy told me how much she loved me.

FIVE

JANE

"Mum," I sang to the computer screen, following it up with a pointed look. "I'm fine. Would you stop worrying."

"You look tired. Slightly green, love. Are you sure you're all right?"

"I just had a little too much good food last night." I rubbed my belly, hoping my cheeks weren't flaming. I didn't want to admit that I gorged myself on a divine array of desserts. The moans coming from our table were orgasmic as Harry and I relished each spoonful of decadence.

Best meal ever.

The only throwback was the tummy ache chaser. We hobbled back to the hotel, already feeling ill before we parted ways. I wriggled and squirmed through the night and was pretty sure I wouldn't be eating anything for at least twenty-four hours.

"So where exactly are you now?" Mum's face disappeared as she tipped up her iPad and gave me a nice view of the Monet print on the wall.

"Tilt your screen, Mum. I can only see your forehead."

"Oh!" She brought herself back into view and I smiled at her.

"I'm in Paris, staying at this gorgeous boutique hotel. It's so pretty. I want to check out the Latin Quarter today, and then I'm not sure what the rest of my week holds. I'm going to spend some time looking over guidebooks and figuring out the rest of my trip."

"Right." Mum forced a smile. "So, you embarked on this adventure with no plans? Jane, that's so unlike you."

"Well, I do have a plan." I shrugged, holding my breath as I lifted up my list. "You know back when we moved to LA and I tried to run away because I was miserable and you made me write that list?"

Mum nodded.

"I've started a new one." I didn't hold it too close to the screen. I didn't want her freaking out over the skydiving or skinny-dipping bullet points. "I think it's going to help me find my way."

Mum's eyes glimmered with pride. "I so respect

your courage and bravery, but you have to promise that you'll still be safe."

"I'm being safe," I assured her, again praying that my skin would control itself and not start flashing a red warning. I was totally going to call next time. Screw Skype; it gave away too much.

"Oh, I'm sure you are, but I hate the idea of you traveling abroad all by yourself. Are you sure I shouldn't come and join you? I could help you cross some things off."

"No!" I snapped, probably too sharply.

The hopeful smile dropped off her face, replaced with a wounded puppy look.

Giving her a bashful grin, I downplayed my outburst with a soft explanation. "I need to do this on my own, Mum. I'm trying to figure out how to live again, and I can't keep leaning on you and Dad, and Sarah and Justin. I have to step outside my comfort zone."

She blinked rapidly, shooing away her tears with a sniff. "I'm proud of you, my sweet Georjana. Just make sure you come home in one piece. You hear me?"

"I will, Mum."

Her face crested with a look of agony. "I would have borne your pain in a heartbeat if I could have."

"I know." I swallowed, my throat clogged with sadness. "But I'm glad you still have Dad, and I'll always have Blake." I tapped my chest. "In here."

She beamed at me, kissing her fingers and touching the screen. "Well, you two enjoy Paris, then."

"We will," I choked out, clicking off my iPad as soon as she hung up. Dropping it on my lap, I gazed out the window and rubbed the spot above my heart. "So, what do you think, Blake? You liking Paris so far?"

He didn't answer.

I was sane enough to know I'd only ever sense his presence, never hear it, feel it brush against my skin, or hold me close at night.

Blake may have been in Paris with me, but not in the same capacity as Harry, and it made me slide the iPad off my lap and scurry down to breakfast.

*****

The glass-roofed sunroom was at the back of the hotel, looking out over a well-kept lawn no bigger than my classroom. Harry was sitting by the open doors, reading a paper and sipping from a delicate teacup. A croissant was on the plate in front of him, but he'd yet to touch it.

By the pale tone of his skin and the state of his mussed-up curls, I was guessing he felt as much like dining as I did.

Gliding around the tables, I tucked my summer dress beneath my legs and sat in the cane chair opposite him.

"*Bonjour.*" I tried out what little French I could remember. "*Comment allez-vous?*"

His upper lip curled and he grunted. "*Je me suis senti mieux.*"

My nose wrinkled as I tried to interpret. "I am…? Oh, I don't know."

He smiled, giving me a glimpse of his slightly crooked front teeth. "I've been better."

"Hmm." I tipped my head with a mock smile. "What on earth could be ailing you?"

"Ha-ha," he muttered drily, taking another sip of his tea while I laughed then held my stomach and groaned.

He snickered and lifted his finger at the waitress.

As soon as the woman appeared, he pointed at me and she turned with a smile. "*Qu'est-ce que vous désirez, madame?*"

"*Ah, parlez-vous anglais?*" I winced and gave her a chagrined smile.

She grinned. "Of course, madam. What would you like?"

Her accent was beautiful. "Thank you. Um, could I please just have some tea? Plain, black, weak tea and a slice of toast."

"Whole wheat?" She took the spare menu off the small round table and tucked it under her arm.

"Yes, please."

With an elegant nod, she walked away from the table, and I leaned back with a contended sigh.

"Not bad, Buford. They always like it when you at least try to speak their language."

"She was very nice about it."

Folding his paper shut, he placed it on the table and looked at me. "So, dear Jane, what are we doing today?"

"Well, I thought we could check out the Latin Quarter and then I don't know. Should we do the Eiffel Tower and all the touristy spots?"

He grimaced and shook his head. "Give us a geezer at that list of yours."

I pulled it from my pocket and handed it over.

He gently unfolded it and scanned the contents, his eyebrows lifting in surprise. "You haven't added *eat the most indulgent meal known to mankind*."

I laughed. "Well, we've already done that."

"Exactly." He handed the paper back and tapped the empty space at the bottom of the page. "You must add it then cross it off."

My heart melted for a moment. He had no idea, and I wasn't sure if I would ever be brave enough to admit it, but I did that kind of thing all the time. When I was working at school, if I did a task that wasn't on my list, I'd always scribble it down and then run a line through it.

Pulling the pen from my handbag, I wrote his words exactly, then crossed it off with a flourish.

"Now doesn't that feel good?"

All I could do was give him a dopey grin.

He took the sheet back, looked it over, and then glanced at his watch. "With only thirteen days to go, I say we leave Paris tomorrow and head south."

"South. What's south?"

He gave me a pitiful look. "You honestly don't know? Aren't you a schoolteacher? Surely you know the geography of this continent."

"Um…" I winced, my cheeks growing warm.

"Good Lord!" His eyes bulged. "Well, I'm not

52

going to tell you, and you have to promise me you won't look it up on a map."

"Why not?"

"Because it will be the perfect chance to surprise you."

I made a face. "I don't like surprises."

"Hey, you said you wanted to see where the road takes you, and so you shall. Now promise me, Jane." He held out his pinky finger.

My face bunched with a skeptical frown. "A pinky promise? How old are we again?"

"They are the most sacred of promises. Now, I really must insist."

I giggled, loving the expression on his face. For a boy from Rye, he really knew how to put on royal-class airs. I loved his jesting tone and the way he held his nose just so. He was completely charming, and I couldn't resist wrapping my pinky finger around his.

"I promise I will not look at a map."

"Or plan too far ahead. We shall decide each day's events at breakfast with the proviso that they could be changed at a moment's notice."

I grimaced, trying to pull out of the finger hold. I didn't think I was capable of such spontaneity. Jumping in a car with Harry was the most wild, impulsive thing I'd ever done, and there he was, making me promise to make the whole trip like that.

Harry tightened his grip. "Come on, Jane, be a sport. You're trying to reinvent yourself, remember?"

I gave in with a sigh, my shoulders drooping as I shook on the promise and agreed to make the next two weeks a trip of surprises. I didn't know how I'd manage, but it felt good nonetheless. Excitement warred with nerves, making it hard to eat my toast when it arrived.

Buttering the bread to the very edges like I always did, I picked at the crumbs on the plate, my leg bobbing beneath the table as Harry read me some of the French articles from the paper.

By the time my tea was finished, he had me laughing over some celebrity and her poodle. I didn't know if he was distracting me on purpose or not, but it didn't matter. I was confident Harry's charm could probably get me to do anything.

And that part should have scared me the most.

SIX

HARRY

I checked Jane's profile out of the corner of my eye as we drove into Spain. At first she didn't notice, but then she spotted a sign and her eyes narrowed.

"Spain," she murmured, then whipped to face me. "Spain! Of course. I knew that."

"You did not know that," I teased her.

She blushed and gave away her lie. I couldn't help stealing a second glance at her rosy complexion, glimpsing it fade back to white to reveal her pale freckles again.

As we headed down the coastline the overcast

sky opened up, drenching Yambi and making her little wipers work overtime. They squeaked back and forth and I slowed to a crawl, negotiating the road with care.

After twenty minutes of gripping the wheel, my fingers were getting sore. "I say we find the first hotel we can and just pull in for the night. I know it's only midday, but this storm feels like it's going to hang around for a while. I don't like driving in this kind of weather."

Jane's head bobbed. "Sounds good to me."

Pointing at my phone, I asked her to do a quick search for accommodations in San Sebastián, and we soon found a quaint little inn with a view of the bay. There was only one hitch...if you chose to consider it that way.

"Only one room available, sir," the woman informed me in her thick Spanish accent. "Very busy over summer."

"Yes, I understand. Uh…"

I exchanged a tentative glance with Jane and raised my eyebrows in question. Her lips pursed to the side as she turned and looked through the front window at where Yambi was parked. The rain was torrential, pelting onto the tiled entranceway.

She glanced back and gave us both a brave smile. "We'll make it work. Thank you."

Tucking her wet, frizzing hair behind her ear, she remained quiet while I checked us in and then led the way to the room.

It was a small space with bright green walls. A tartan yellow and purple duvet covered the small double bed. There was a couch at the end, which I offered to sleep on.

"I can take it. I'm shorter."

"Jane." I shook my head. "I have been working overtime to make sure you don't feel like I'm trying to flirt with you. I haven't opened doors or carried your bag, I haven't offered to pay for any meals, but I cross the line at making you take the couch. Please, let me play my gentleman card on this one. I won't be able to sleep a wink otherwise."

Her green eyes warmed with a smile when she nodded and mouthed, "Thank you."

My insides curled with affection as I gazed at her. She was growing more beautiful every day, and it made me nervous. We'd met less than a week ago. Technically she was still in the stranger zone, yet she wasn't, because being with her was so incredibly easy.

Brushing past her, I walked to the windows and stared out at the darkened sky. A flash of lightning lit the air followed by a loud rumble of thunder. "Blimey. Zeus must be pretty aggro about something."

Jane laughed, bending down to unzip her bag and pull out a change of clothes. "I'm gonna have a shower. Then maybe we could…" She looked around the room, and then her eyes landed on my computer bag. "You have any movies on your computer?"

"Uh, yeah." I was slow to answer, knowing that all I had was my collection of sci-fi and fantasy movies. I barely knew any girls who were into that kind of thing.

"When I was a kid and it rained like this on the weekend, my dad and I would always sit down for a movie marathon. You got anything marathon-worthy?"

I winced and crossed my arms. "Um, just a few sci-fi type…"

"Any *Star Wars*?"

My eyebrows lifted at the eager expression on her face. "Yeah, all seven."

Her lips lifted into a smile as she checked her watch. "I'd say we could fit in the original three. Maybe even have time for *The Force Awakens*, don't you?"

I couldn't speak for a moment then blinked and whispered, "You like *Star Wars*?"

"Oh, yeah. Huge fan. I love all those types of movies. *Star Trek*, *Aliens*, *Terminator*… the Marvel Universe." She tipped her head back. "I *love* the Marvel movies."

And I love you, I thought.

Thank God I didn't whisper the words aloud. I was too surprised to do anything more than bob my head and give her a stupid grin.

"I'll shower quickly." Her eyes sparkled and she winked at me before spinning on her heel and heading into the bathroom.

I clutched a hand to my chest and dipped my knees.

"Hey, do you think this place will have room service?" Jane called from behind the closed door.

"I can call and find out."

"Order us a bunch of comfort food, will ya? Let's be slobs today."

"Really, truly love you," I mumbled as I grabbed the phone and dialed the front desk.

Forty minutes later I was stretched out on the bed, sharing an array of delicious Spanish food with Jane. The *Star Wars* music started up and I felt my insides buzz like they always did. I'd seen the movie a hundred times, but I still loved the thrill of reading that yellow writing and getting pulled into a galaxy far, far away.

By the time Luke Skywalker and Han Solo were rescuing Princess Leia, the bowls and plates had been licked clean. Moving them to the floor, I stretched back on the mound of pillows and rested my hand beneath my head. Jane shifted around, lying on her side and letting her bare feet dangle off the edge of the bed. Her damp hair rested on the pillow beside me. I could smell the citrus scent and wondered what it was doing to my body.

I hadn't felt anything like it in such a long time. Unearthing those desires should have sent me reeling. I should have been pulling away, jumping off the bed, finding something better to do.

But I couldn't, even if I tried.

In that moment, I was so content I never wanted to move again.

SEVEN

JANE

We'd been on the road just over a week when I faced my first 'I'm not sure I can do this' challenge. I was on a holiday high. After our rain-induced movie marathon, we awoke the next morning to sunshine, spent the day at the beach, and then traveled through the evening to Barcelona. I loved the vibrant city with its unique architecture, blending the old and the new. I struggled to leave, so we squeezed in an extra night, then headed through Seville and were on our way to Portugal. Every day I couldn't believe I was actually living my list.

I'd crossed off learning to surf—I was terrible at it.

We'd ridden horses along the beach—loved it, could do it every day for the rest of my life.

I'd read *The Great Gatsby*—not bad.

We stayed up late the night before watching *Gone with the Wind*—I loved it, although I couldn't decide if I had because of the movie or because my arm had been pressed against Harry's the whole time we watched. His long legs had been stretched out on my bed, crossed at the ankles. I'd studied the shape of his large, manly feet resting next to my short, stubby toes. Swirls of his deodorant had tickled my nostrils. It was a musky scent that I kind of enjoyed. Just having a masculine presence that close to me again had been nothing but comforting. It reminded me of Blake...of how much I missed being in a relationship.

Our *Star Wars* movie marathon, the conversations over meal times, the easy laughter, the funny quips and banter between Harry and me. It was all so easy, so natural. The endearing Brit was the perfect distraction, but I could never fully forget Blake. He was always there inside my heart, reminding me why I could never fall in love again.

Harry was a great companion, and that was all he ever could be.

Standing on the edge of the rock, I peered over the side and grimaced. "I don't think I can do this."

"Jane, if you have any hope of jumping out of a plane one day, you have to be able to jump off a rock into a pool of water."

"But it's so high," I squeaked.

We'd discovered the sanctuary about an hour ago by taking a wrong turn and going with it. The road had gotten narrower and bumpier, but in spite of my jittery complaints, we bravely continued and found the oasis. It was a deep, crystal clear pool surrounded by rocks with a waterfall running into it. I wouldn't have been surprised if we were on private property, but I was too inspired by the beauty to care.

After we'd donned our swimsuits we ran to the water's edge, but Harry stopped me from jumping in, pointing to the climbable rocks. I hesitated, chewing on my lips while he quickly checked the depth of the water.

His head popped back up, and he flicked the wet hair off his face. "It's perfect! Come on." He swam to the rocks, and I foolishly followed him.

Harry leaned out to look down at the crystal blue water. "I'd say about thirty feet. That's a high-dive board at the Olympics, I think. Imagine being able to write that on your list, then cross it off." He gave me an impressed grin.

I snickered. He'd been making me do that a lot. Putting me in list-worthy situations.

"You know, Jane, you could actually be crossing off more than one thing if you do this. The water's clear enough to see your toes, and there's a waterfall small enough that you can swim beneath it. And if you want to go for the triple whammy, you could take that bikini off and do it naked." He crossed his arms with a mischievous wink.

I blinked, my insides going crazy as I tried to figure a way out of it. But then I snapped my eyes closed and forced myself to stop thinking.

If Blake were there, he'd be yanking his swim shorts off without a moment's hesitation, laughing at the sky then cannonballing into the water.

"Okay," I blurted, shocked I'd managed to say it. My eyes popped open and I gasped. I took in Harry's surprised smile then narrowed my eyes at him. "But you have to do it too."

"What?" He laughed, stepping away from me. "It's not *my* list."

"Yes, but you came on this trip to help me with my quest, and I don't have the guts to do this alone. I need you, Harry. Please, do this with me."

My words made him flinch. His face bunched with a frown and he took a step back from me, like I'd just hit him with a stick or something.

"What's the matter?" My belly did a little flip as I watched him. What could I have possibly said to give him a reaction like that? My mind raced back through the last few minutes, analyzing my words and tone.

His jaw clenched, and he wouldn't look at me. With a stiff shake of his head, he sniffed and forced a jovial smile.

I saw right through it.

Crossing my arms, I tipped my head and stared at him. I desperately wanted to know what was running through his mind. My words had triggered some memory...some kind of regret. His fake smile couldn't hide that haunted look in his eyes. Multiple questions sat inside my mouth, anxious to burst out of me, but I held them all back because I knew what he was going to say.

"No histories, Jane. Please…" His voice caught, and I felt my heart begin to crack. Whatever he was remembering hurt him, and I recognized—*felt*—the sadness sweeping over his expression.

"I'm sorry," I murmured, backpedaling as fast as I could. "Let's, um…" Shaking my head, I looked to the blue sky and was about to start climbing back down the rocks. "We should go. This is probably private property and—"

"No," he croaked. "I want to stay."

I caught the edge of my bottom lip with my teeth and studied him. Fear pulsed through me at the sudden thought that maybe he was about to open up, to try to smooth things over with a painful story from his past, but I didn't want that.

The trip was about fun spontaneity. I couldn't handle grief. I didn't want to cry with Harry. I didn't want him finding out about Blake! If he told me his sad secret, would he then expect to hear mine?

Maybe the whole trip was a bad idea. Should I really be traveling with a stranger? What if his past was checkered? What had he done to cause that look of regret?

I swallowed and jittered, inching across the hard rock, ready for a quick escape. "It's okay, Harry. I don't mind. I don't need to jump. I don't have to cross things off my list every day. It's really not a problem."

"Jane." He tried to stop the nervous drivel spewing from my mouth.

"It's only a list anyway. It's hardly important in the scheme of things, I mean this is just—"

"Jane!"

I bit my lips together, my cheeks tinging pink after his loud bark.

He softened his tone with a charming smile, the one that somehow warmed me without my say-so. I stared into his hazel eyes and was yet again won over by his tenderness. The man had a good heart, there was no hiding it. Whatever he'd done in his past couldn't have been that bad, surely.

"Get back over here, Lady Jane. We're going to erase the last few moments from our minds. I'm sorry about that blip, I just…Your words. The way you said them reminded me of…" He ran a hand through his curls and shook his head. "Of course I'll do this with you."

"You don't have to," I whispered.

His gaze was serious when he looked at me, drinking me in as if I was someone else for just a moment. "I want to." He blinked, his eyes clearing then instantly filling with his trademark twinkle. "Besides, I'm hardly about to pass up a chance to see you naked."

I jerked to a stop, gaping at him before blinking indignantly. "Excuse me?"

He snickered, sliding his thumbs into the waistband of his swim shorts and acting like he hadn't just had a sadness blackout.

"What is happening right now?"

"We're going to jump into that pool of luscious water completely starkers." He winked at me. "So, come on then. Get your gears off."

Biting my lips together, I gave him one more dubious frown. He wiggled his eyebrows and started sliding his shorts down. I spun away from him and, with quivering fingers, untied my bikini. I couldn't believe I was actually doing it. My heart was thumping so hard and fast I thought I might faint. The only guy to ever see me fully naked was Blake. He'd been my first…and my last.

I closed my eyes and reminded myself of that before slowly turning. My eyes crept open, an appreciative smile forming on my lips as I checked out Harry. I'd seen him shirtless multiple times throughout our week. He was hot, there was no denying it. Girls checked him out on the beach. His defined torso caught several hungry gazes. He wasn't the bulky, body-builder type but had a long, lean, athletic kind of build. I liked his arms the best. They had a nice shape to them—the curve of his bicep, the way his forearms rippled when he lifted our packs into the back of his nan's Bambino.

My gaze traveled over his abs, tracing the two lines that dipped toward his manhood. And it was an impressive manhood. His thighs were pretty nice too, strong and muscular. My insides fired with desire, but I swallowed the feeling away. I wasn't into Harry Tindal. He was my friend and would be nothing more. Ever.

Even so, I couldn't stop checking him out.

I wondered if he was checking me out as well,

but I was too afraid to look him in the eye. An awkward silence started to settle around us, but thankfully Harry whisked it away with his humor.

"So, thoughts?" He bent his knee and started pulling body-builder poses, flexing his muscles until they quivered, and growling like a model from *Zoolander*.

Laughter burst out of me, killing the tension and uncoiling the knot in my stomach.

"I know. I know you thought Hercules was just a myth…" He ran his hands down the sides of his body and struck another pose. "Sorry to shatter the illusion for you, but as you can see, demigods are in fact real."

I was laughing so hard I could barely stand up straight. I hated to think what my naked body looked like. My breasts were probably jiggling, and he was probably getting a pretty decent view of my downstairs while I tipped my head to the sky and laughed.

"Just jump in, you big loser." I giggled out the words.

He grinned at me and held out his arm toward the edge of the rock. "After you, Aphrodite."

The way he called me the goddess of beauty sent a delicious shiver curling down my spine. I gave him an excited, nervous grin, then stepped up to the edge, my toes curling over the lip of the rock. My body started to shake, my knees feeling weak and pathetic as I stared down at the water.

Then Harry's fingers slipped around my hand. "Together on Geronimo," he murmured.

"One…" I started.

"Two…" he continued.

"Geronimo!" we shouted together. I screamed as we launched into the air and started falling.

I pointed my toes last minute and plunged into the pool. The sound of the waterfall became muffled as water shot up my nose and filled my ears. I kicked hard and popped into the sunshine, gulping in a lungful of air. Harry popped up beside me and whooped!

"That was amazing!" I yelled, feeling a buzzy giddiness like nothing I'd experienced before. Jumping off those rocks was liberating, exhilarating…and I couldn't stop laughing.

"Can you see your toes?"

I looked into the water and laughed some more. The water warped my body, but I could see all the way down my legs to the blue polish on my toes. "Yes!" I screamed and let out a joyous shout. Tipping my head back, I closed my eyes against the sun and floated on the water. It lapped against my naked skin, cool and refreshing.

It was easy to forget that I was baring all to the man treading water beside me. I was too lost in the magic of the hot sun on my face and the cool water surrounding my body. The waterfall ran with a peaceful consistency that could have lulled me into a dream-like doze.

But my peaceful bob in the water was not meant to be.

I heard the whoosh first, then gasped as my face was covered by a wave of water. Spluttering, my legs dropped back into the pool, and I started pushing water back at Harry before I'd even opened my eyes.

When the splashing had died down, I scrubbed a hand over my face and peeked my eyes open. Harry's gaze was sweet and warm, the way it always was. I have to admit, that blip on the top of the rock was easy to forget when he looked at me like that.

It made me realize how much I didn't care about his past. The man in the pool of water with me was a good person, someone I loved spending time with. And as curious as I was, our histories didn't matter. It wouldn't change the fact that I was crossing things off my list and having more fun than I ever imagined I could.

"Come on, you." He tipped his head toward the waterfall and started swimming.

I got a nice view of his butt as he kicked and swam away from me. It was round and taut with a dimple on each cheek. My insides stirred with desire again, my throat constricting as thoughts of Blake tickled the back of my mind.

"You're still with me, right?" I whispered to him, waiting for that familiar sense of peace to curl through me.

I didn't really feel it and kept treading water, waiting for more.

I looked to the sky, wondering if Blake's eyes were on me. How would he have felt about me stripping naked in front of another man?

"I love you," I murmured. "Only you."

"Jane, come on!" Harry shouted. "This is amazing!"

My eyes shot to the waterfall, and for a second I thought about pulling back, racing for my towel to cover myself, but...

I couldn't do it.

I was on this trip to live for Blake and myself. Swimming under a waterfall was on my list. It didn't matter who was with me or what I was wearing. I had a quest to fulfill, and if I didn't swim for that waterfall, I'd regret it.

Closing my eyes, I whispered to my love again, "Let's go."

But I couldn't help wondering as I swam for Harry if I was leaving Blake behind.

I didn't know if I was ready to do that.

EIGHT

HARRY

I couldn't get the thought of Jane's naked body out of my mind. She was beautiful—her curves, the milky color of her skin, those perfect breasts. It took every ounce of concentration not to grow an erection right in front of her.

I didn't want to think of her as anything more than a friend. That was not what the trip was about. We were there to discover ourselves, to move away from pasts that were haunting us. I had no idea what Jane's was. I'd had my fair share of guesses, but she'd said nothing concrete enough for me to know.

I'd given her nothing either, except for my little blip on the rock. Tammy had said exactly the same thing to me when she'd wanted to get married and I'd refused her. We hadn't needed marriage to be together. Things had been perfect as they were...until I refused one too many times and lost her completely. As I'd stood on that rock, battling regret, I'd come so close to telling Jane the truth, but her pale skin and panicky retreat shut me up. I'd never been there for Tammy the way I should have been, but I would be for Jane.

Tammy would remain my secret not to share. I didn't want to bring her into the equation. It was too painful, too guilt-inducing. I knew logically I wasn't the only one to blame, but I'd played a significant part in losing her, and I couldn't stomach the idea of what Jane would think of me if she knew what a coward I'd been.

I'd made a vow to never put myself in a position like that again. Love was too painful. But the longer I spent with Jane, the more I realized that I was a fool. Was denying my attraction, the easy banter we had between us, the comfortable silences, the way it all felt so natural really the right thing to do? I was falling for this American girl...and I wasn't sure how much longer I could deny it.

"Well, you scrub up nicely." Jane appeared beside me.

I'd been so lost in my thoughts I hadn't even noticed her approach.

I leaned away to check out the green dress she'd purchased at the market that morning. It had one of those skirts that floated around her knees. The thing we both liked the most was the intricate gold design stitched into the bodice and skirt hem. It looked Arabian with tiny gold beads outlining the swirls and leaf-shaped patterns.

"Stunning," I murmured.

"I know, right? My friend Sarah is going to go crazy for this dress."

Jane sat down opposite me, oblivious to the fact I'd been thinking about her rather than the dress when I murmured *stunning*.

"She actually designed my—" Her voice cut off and she gave me a tight smile, her eyes glassing over. She picked up her menu and hid behind it while I resisted the urge to probe for more.

She'd probably mutter, "No histories," anyway, just like I had.

I cleared my throat and perused the dinner choices. "I've already ordered a red for us to share."

"Oh, cool. Was it the one we had a few nights back at the vineyard?"

"It is."

"You're a smart man."

"I know."

She snickered at my light joke but still wouldn't show me her face. I was desperate to know what Sarah had designed for her and why she couldn't tell me about it, but it was pointless to try to find out. More than anything, I wanted to keep the trip light and fun. So far, it'd been exactly that. We had three nights left before we had to drive back to Rye, and I wasn't about to ruin the end of our trip with awkward, emotional conversations.

The waiter came over, and we ordered our meal. After eating every meal with her for the last several days, I could have confidently ordered on her behalf. She had very similar tastes to mine, and I was struck once again by how easy it was to be with her.

She'd methodically been trying to crush every one of my doubts that falling in love again was a bad idea.

I felt like I'd found my other half.

How could I not fall for her?

But...

Tammy twirled through my brain, her luscious locks of blonde hair, her sweet strawberry scent, the taste of her lips, and that smile that could have made me do anything...well, almost anything.

I closed my eyes and swallowed, turning away so Jane couldn't see my expression.

We were at an open-air restaurant, seated at a small table on the edge of the large, round balcony. Music played to my right, entertaining the couples swaying in the center of the cobbled eatery. The faint smell of sea salt floated in the air. The nearby ocean was an inky patch of darkness, the sandy beach framed by lights from the bordering houses and restaurants.

I was sitting in paradise across from a beautiful girl, and all I could feel was an aching sadness, a bleak regret. If life had been fair, if I'd been the man I was supposed to be, Tammy would be sitting across from me. She'd be chirping away in her speedy voice, going over everything we'd done that day, linking her fingers and resting her chin on her hands.

But she wasn't.

And she never would be.

Turning away from the thought that always felt like a punch to the face, I focused back on Jane. She was watching the couples dancing, her lips softly curled at the edges.

The band was performing an acoustic version of "The Edge of Glory." It sounded great. I bobbed my head while the beat worked through me, and then I glanced at Jane.

"Want to dance with me?"

Jane's head swiveled in my direction, her eyes wide at first, but then they narrowed and she nodded. "Sure."

I held out my hand, and she took it like it was the most natural thing in the world.

Because it was.

My heart double-thumped as I pulled her against me and we started to dance. Her hips swayed and we easily found a rhythm, getting lost in the music.

Her face was bright when I twirled her beneath my arm before resting my hand on her lower back. She fitted perfectly in my arms. I liked the smell of her hair—a citrus scent, so fresh and alluring. Her thick locks tickled the side of my face, and I couldn't help rubbing them between my fingers as she leaned against me.

I closed my eyes, resting my cheek on her head and feeling like we'd been doing this for years.

The song finished but we stayed where we were. Jane's fingers squeezed my hand as the next song began. Being a huge Ed Sheeran fan, I recognized the "Kiss Me" cover immediately. Tammy and I used to lie in bed listening to his music all the time.

The thought should have made me move away from Jane, but I couldn't. We started swaying in time to the music, our feet barely moving as we basically just hugged on the dance floor. Running my arm up her back, I pressed her closer. She turned her head, resting it against my shoulder and brushing the tip of her nose across the racing pulse in my neck.

She felt just right in my arms, like she'd been meant to be there all along.

I didn't understand it, but that wasn't enough to stop me from dipping my head and caressing my lips across her smooth cheek. I pressed a kiss against her ear. Her head lifted off my shoulder, her fingers playing with the short curls at the nape of my neck. Her green eyes were so wide and open, searching my gaze in question.

I answered before fear stopped me.

Leaning forward, I pressed my mouth to hers, closing my eyes and relishing the softness of her lips. She pushed back, running her fingers into my hair and tipping her head. I took that as permission to deepen the kiss. Parting my lips, I brushed the tip of my tongue against her top lip—a quiet little knock for entry.

She responded, her breath mingling with mine as she let me in.

Her tongue was warm and tasted faintly of the peppermints she was always sucking between meals. I ran my tongue along it, savoring the flavor, the sensation, lost in the magic of kissing a girl I cared for.

I hadn't done that in a really long time, and I'd forgotten how much better it was.

Until it ended.

With a small gasp, Jane tore her mouth from mine. "No." She shook her head and stumbled out of my embrace.

Covering her mouth with quivering fingers, she looked at me with wide, glassy eyes before fleeing the dance floor.

The couple next to me turned to give me a quizzical look but I ignored them, walking back to our table in a slight daze.

Her eyes, the way they shone like that. It reminded me of Tammy, the last time I'd seen her. She'd been standing in our doorway, begging me...and I'd shrugged and told her she was asking too much.

If only I'd said yes.

I could have wiped that look off her face, made her happy.

Instead I'd kissed goodbye the last chance I'd ever have with her.

Scrubbing a hand over my face, I stopped at the table, staring out at the black mass of water. Thoughts of Tammy were pushed aside by Jane.

I didn't want to make the same mistakes I had in the past.

I should have fought for Tammy. Tried a little harder. Was I honestly ready to pull another Harry, shy away from the difficult conversations so I didn't have to feel anything more than lighthearted humor?

Pinching my lower lip, I let out a sigh and headed left in search of Jane.

Thankfully I found her easily. She was resting against the marble railing, in the next tier down. The wind was making tendrils of her hair dance across her face. She tucked them behind her ear, then slashed her finger under her eye.

Sliding my hands into my pockets, I cleared my throat so she knew I was coming before I ambled over to her. Resting my legs against the railing, I stared across the houses and out to that inky black sea.

"I'm sorry if I crossed a line."

"No, it's okay. I..." She shook her head and sighed.

Her lips bunched as she fought a fresh wave of emotion.

I kept my voice soft and non-confronting. "Jane, I know we said no pasts, but do you mind my asking if you're married, or getting over someone?"

She let out a wispy, sad laugh, then sniffed. "No. I mean ye—I mean, I don't..." She squeezed her eyes shut and huffed out the rest. "I was nearly married, but..." She shook her head. "You're the first person I've kissed since him and I just..."

Hearing those words out of her mouth was a comfort more than anything. I got it. I understood completely what she was going through. If she was anything like me, her insides were a mashed-up mess. He must have been someone pretty special, just like my Tammy.

Jane's quiet sniffles brought me back to her side. "You must think I'm pathetic."

I ran a hand up her back and then lightly patted her shoulder, not wanting the touch to be anything more than friendly. "Not at all. Again, I'm sorry for kissing you, but I just couldn't resist. I'm blaming the dress, actually."

A smile tugged at her lips but it was wonky and weak. "I'm flattered."

"Please do be. The dress really is beautiful." I winked so she knew I was actually talking about her.

She of course got my double meaning, the way she so often did. Her cheeks fired red. Not even the fact we were standing in a pale beam of moonlight could hide the color of her skin.

I laughed and tucked a lock of hair behind her ear. "Don't worry. This trip is not going to get awkward. We said no sex and I meant it." I lifted my chin and squinted up at the sky. "Don't even want to." I stuck out my tongue and made a disgusted face, hoping for a laugh.

I got one...and a slap on the arm.

"Watch it." She pointed at me, her eyebrow peaked.

I grinned and spun to face her, resting my butt

on the railing and enjoying the way the pale light made her green eyes glow. The tears had added to their vibrancy, making her more beautiful than I'd ever seen her. It was enough to steal a man's breath.

But I couldn't let it, and so I tuned in to the music above, grateful the band had moved on to a more upbeat set.

"Can't Stop The Feeling" was playing and I pointed to the stairs. "Let's get up there and dance like five-year-olds."

Jane's nose wrinkled. "What?"

"Yeah, let's be crazy." I took her hand and dragged her up the stairs. Stopping on the edge of the dance floor, I pointed to the middle and said, "I dare you to go right into the middle and dance like you're a five-year-old."

"You are insane."

"I know." I nodded. "Ready?"

She let out a reluctant groan, then grimaced and squeaked, "One…"

"Two…"

"Geronimo!" We laughed the words together, then ran onto the dance floor and started flailing around like kids. I waved my arms in the air while she jumped on her feet and giggled, her body writhing around like a floppy rag doll.

People stopped to watch us, no doubt assuming we were drunk, but we didn't care. Our crazy joy was contagious. The dancers nearby started laughing with us, and a couple even joined in.

Jane's smile was like a spotlight—mesmerizing

and making my heart do things it hadn't done
...maybe ever.

NINE

JANE

Two weeks.

I couldn't believe it had come to an end so quickly.

I'd laughed more in that short time than I had in an entire year. Harry's humor, his funny little quips, made the trip so easy and light. We'd talked about so much and not enough. We'd experienced so many cool things. My list was covered with lines, and I wasn't sure how I was going to keep crossing them off without him.

But I was due back home.

I had a life waiting for me in America.

And Harry had a life in Rye.

We'd agreed from the outset that we'd live life to the max and then go our separate ways. That was why the trip worked so well, because there was an end. We couldn't do it forever.

After everything I'd gone through with Blake, I didn't think I could do anything for forever.

The Bambino doors clunked closed. I ran my hand over the roof of the little car, loving its sunshine yellow coating. I thought it'd be a cramped nightmare, but Harry was right. My travel story was made ten times cooler by going in Yambi.

"I'll miss you," I whispered to the car before following Harry to my rental.

I pressed the key and the car unlocked before he reached it. I made sure to study Harry's arms as he lifted my pack into the trunk.

He really did have delicious arms.

I could still feel them around me when we danced, the pressure of his fingers on my back as he held me close. I'd dreamed about it every night since it'd happened, but he'd been true to his word and hadn't tried it on again.

I was grateful...and disappointed.

I frowned and reprimanded myself. "Grateful. You're grateful," I muttered under my breath.

Ambling to a stop, I leaned against the hood of the car and gave Harry a closed-mouth smile as he paused in front of me. Sliding his hands into his pockets, he squinted against the sunlight and mirrored my grin.

"Well, I hope you're feeling thoroughly

discovered."

I snickered and looked down at my fingers while I fidgeted with the car keys. I couldn't tell him I wasn't. I mean, I was, but I also stood there feeling incredibly lost, because I was about to leave him…and be all alone again.

Except for Blake.

I forced the reminder through my head. I still had Blake. He'd always be with me.

"Well, I guess you should get going. Don't want you missing that flight."

"No." I shook my head, biting my lips against telling him where I was flying to.

It seemed strange that he knew so much about me, yet so little.

We'd avoided all those specific details and basically stuck to who we were on the inside. I felt like Harry knew a huge part of my heart and soul yet still didn't know who I was.

It was all so confusing, and I couldn't help a frown.

"Oh, come here, you." Harry didn't wait for permission; he just scooped me into his arms, lifting me off the ground before placing me back on my tiptoes and holding me tight against him.

I dug my fingers into his shoulders and pressed my lips against his shirt.

Neither of us wanted to let go.

And I didn't know who'd have the courage to back out first.

"I think I'm in love with you." Harry whispered the words so softly I wasn't sure if I was imagining them.

My insides froze, my eyes popping wide as I stared over his shoulder at the old brick building across the street.

I had two ways of dealing with his words.

And the coward in me pretended not to hear them.

"I had a wonderful time." I kissed his cheek and pulled out of the embrace. Squeezing his arms, my mind flashed with an image of his naked body by the waterfall. I swallowed down my desire and stepped back, bumping into the car and letting out a shaky laugh. "You were a great travel partner, and I'm so grateful for everything you did for me."

He forced a bright smile, but his eyes said something else. I really hoped he assumed I hadn't heard him. He obviously didn't have the courage to repeat himself, and I turned for my door before he found it.

Shutting the door for me, he leaned down, and I lowered the window so he could say his final goodbye.

"You take care of yourself, Georjana. May you get everything your heart desires." His smile was heartfelt yet bleak. I gazed into his hazel eyes and had to resist the urge to lean forward and kiss him.

If I did, I'd never be able to leave.

And I couldn't stay, because I was in love with another man. Sure, he was dead, but that didn't matter. Blake owned my heart.

Harry and I only worked because we were in this magical holiday bubble. I couldn't bring him into my normal life. I couldn't fall in love again. I wasn't willing to risk it.

Besides, he had his nan to look after and I had a life in LA. I couldn't just ditch my students and move to England!

Turning the key with stiff, awkward fingers, I gripped the wheel and stared at the road before me.

"I'll never forget you, Harry." I sucked in a breath and accelerated away before he could say anything more to turn me.

Tears filled my eyes as I headed out of Rye, but I bit my bottom lip and told myself I was doing the right thing.

It was nearly a three-hour trip to Heathrow Airport, and by the time I finally got there the mantra was a painful earworm in my brain, chipping away at my resolve and tainting what had been two of the best weeks of my life.

TEN

HARRY

I stood outside The Whistle Inn until Mrs. Pimberton walked up and asked me if I was feeling okay. I nodded, forced a smile, and then petted her doe-eyed King Charles Spaniel. My insides were quiet and ash-like, crumbling to pieces as I drove home to Nan's.

I wanted to be annoyed with myself for not telling Jane again, but when she hadn't heard me, I figured it was a sign. Maybe I wasn't meant to love her.

We'd just had the best two weeks of our lives, but if we tried to turn it into something more, it no doubt wouldn't work. Love didn't last.

At least not for me.

Fear had held me back in the past, or maybe it was complacency. I thought Tammy had been a sure thing. I didn't need to marry her to prove I loved her.

As far as I was concerned, marriage didn't mean a thing.

It didn't for my parents, anyway.

Tammy never got it though. We'd been together a year when she started making hints about it. Two years later she told it to me straight—*I need you, Harry. Please, do this with me.*

I thought she was being overly dramatic and just shrugged her off.

And then I never saw her again.

My throat was thick when I tried to swallow, my jaw aching when I clenched it. Watching Jane drive away brought it all back again. The loss. The aching hole left behind.

Parking the car, I unloaded my gear and trudged inside. Nan was in the lounge, her nose buried in a book, her forehead wrinkled in concentration. Her hands trembled when she slowly turned the page, but it didn't seem to bother her.

In spite of my unsettled innards, I had to smile. Nan was the sweetest thing on the planet. There was no doubt about it.

"Hey, Nan," I greeted softly, resting against the wooden doorframe.

"Oh, hello, love." She placed the book in her lap

and stretched her arms wide.

Dropping my pack, I maneuvered around the furniture and bent down to kiss her.

"You all right?"

She patted my shoulder and gave me a loud kiss on the cheek. "Good as gold, darling. You made good time back."

"Yeah, well…" I shrugged, standing tall and sliding my hands into my pockets. "She had a flight to catch."

Nan's wrinkled face filled with compassion.

I cleared my throat and turned away from that wise old gaze. Clapping my hands together, I gave them a rub and headed for the stairs. "Right, better get back to work, then. Got a bit of catching up to do."

"It's okay to be sad, Harry."

I raised my hand to acknowledge her. "Right then, Nan. Just call me if you need anything."

She didn't reply, and I was guessing she'd slumped back in her seat, watching me run down the stairs in denial.

Sad.

I didn't want to feel it.

I didn't want to feel anything.

Throwing my pack on the floor, I kicked it out of the way and stalked to my desk. Gently laying my computer bag on the seat, I took out my laptop and got to work setting it up how I liked it. Within five minutes I was back online and ready to jump into a technological sea where my brain did all the work and my heart could shut down for a while.

Pressing the space bar, I got my music pumping. It'd get me in the right zone.

But it didn't work, because Tammy's favorite song started playing, and I found myself sitting on the floor by the bookshelf staring at a picture of my love while "Somewhere Over the Rainbow" played in the background.

Lifting the white frame off the shelf, I ran my finger over her face.

"So, I, uh… I met someone. Finally. Bet you thought I never would." I blinked, my eyes suddenly burning. "I don't know what it is about her, she's just…" I shrugged. "We laughed a lot. I tried to be exactly what she needed and ended up falling for her. Crazy, isn't it? I didn't think I could ever love anyone again after you, but my heart's telling me something different. I don't even know what to do with it, really. I mean, I tried to tell her that I thought I was in love with her, but she didn't hear me." I shook my head. "Probably for the best, right? I shouldn't be spouting love if I can't follow through with it."

I traced Tammy's smile and winced. "Can't believe I said it anyway. It took me months to find the courage to tell you. I'm so sorry, Tam. I should have told you sooner. I should have told you every day." I sniffed, guilt roaring through me. "I should have asked you to marry me like you wanted." Pressing my forehead against the glass, I sucked in a breath and murmured, "She's gone now. And you're gone, and I should be getting back to work. But I don't know if I can. The last two weeks showed me just how bloody miserable I am without you." My voice cracked. "I miss you, Tammy. I'm sorry I was too late. I'm so sorry."

My wobbly voice petered away, and all I was left with was the soft ukulele strum of Tammy's favorite song and a brain full of bittersweet memories to torture me.

Memories of what I once had, what I'd just experienced, and what I'd let slip through my fingers. Any decent man would have jumped from his bed and raced to the airport, pulled off one of those dramatic airport kisses that made the girls swoon.

But I couldn't chase Jane.

She didn't want me to.

And if I was honest, I didn't know if I had the heart to try.

Losing one woman had been hard enough. If I let myself fall completely in love with Jane, I wasn't sure I'd ever be able to get over her.

The right thing to do was to let her go and move on while I still could.

We'd had our two utopian weeks, and they'd have to be enough.

ELEVEN

JANE

"So your trip was amazing, then?" Sarah probed a little more as she drove me home from the airport.

I nodded and gave her a closed-mouth smile. I was worried if I opened my mouth the truth would spill out, and I didn't want to utter a word until I could figure out what the hell I was feeling.

"Can't believe you were so adventurous." Sarah's eyes sparkled. "I'm so proud of you."

"I'm proud of you too." Patting her leg, I tried to veer the conversation away from me. "You and Justin."

Sarah's smile was pure relief. "I know."

"Glad he came to his senses."

"Me too! Although, he had every right to take his time." Sarah's face crested with sadness and guilt.

Great, so now we're both feeling that way.

I spent the entire flight stressing over the fact I ignored Harry's words. It was mean and rude and...

But I didn't know what to say!

I never expected him to fall in love with me, and I never expected to...

I closed my eyes.

No, I didn't love him.

I was in love with Blake.

I shouldn't have felt guilty at all for ignoring him. I saved us both an awkward conversation.

So why did I feel so restless...and sad?

"Anyway." Sarah shrugged as if trying to bump the nasty business she and Justin went through off her shoulders. "That's in the past and we're moving forward. We're never going to put ourselves through that again. Living without him sucked on so many levels."

"Well, I'm glad you've found your way," I murmured, gazing out the window so she couldn't see my face.

"More importantly, have you found your way?"

I bobbed my head. "Yeah, yeah, I think so."

Sarah expelled a breathy giggle. "Your accent has kicked in big time. You're sounding all British again. Which surprises me because didn't you spend most of your break in Europe? Did you hang out with some British tourists or something?"

I whipped back to look at Sarah, my eyes bulging, but she was too busy wiggling her eyebrows and watching the road to notice my giveaway blush.

Tucking my bangs behind my ear, I turned to look back out the window and scrambled for a casual sounding explanation. "You know me. It only takes an hour of British company to get me speaking like this. The flight attendants were enough." I pushed out a laugh.

"Oh man, I was really hoping you were going to say you met some sexy guy on a beach in Spain or something."

"What?" I squeaked.

Sarah laughed and glanced at me. "Come on, wouldn't that have made a great story? Some European affair to get your blood racing again."

"Sarah Louise Doyle, wash your mouth. I'm not interested in some foreign tryst. I went to figure out how to live on my own."

"And did you?"

I forced my head to bob up and down, although I couldn't deny that I'd failed miserably. I learned to live with Harry…and I absolutely loved it.

Couldn't believe I'd spent all that money to travel halfway around the world only to be right back at square one. I'd forever miss Blake, but now I was missing Harry too.

Leaning back against the headrest, I held in my sigh as my apartment building came into view.

Here I was again, about to start a new school year and wondering how I was going to survive it.

*****

My classroom was empty.

The desks were bunched in groups of four, ready for the students to arrive the following week. I'd redone the walls with new posters, and everything was looking neat and tidy, just the way I liked it. My new students wouldn't keep it that way for long, but I'd do my best.

"To Make You Feel My Love" played from my stereo, filling me with nostalgia. Blake used to serenade me with the song, making me swoon and sigh. Tears would line my lashes, and then we'd kiss and make love.

A year ago, I stood in the same spot, listening to the same song...setting up for a new class, a new life without Blake. I didn't know how I'd survive, but I managed. I wanted my second year to feel different. My Europe quest had been about finding my joy, learning to live like an actual human being.

Well, I'd kind of done that.

After Sarah dropped me home from the airport, I took a shower, then fell into bed and slept until nearly midday. It'd been exactly what I'd needed. A chance not to think. I woke up feeling a little brighter, like maybe I could do this second year at Strantham Academy and not feel like I was suffocating.

Blake and I had our special tree in Rye. We were

joined in spirit, and I had hoped I wouldn't feel so lonely.

But as the days ticked by, I wasn't sure the lonely ache in my chest would be so easily conquered.

While I set up my classroom and listened to our songs, Harry kept walking through my mind. I missed him. I wanted him beside me with his mischievous smile and twinkling eyes. He'd make some joke about one of my posters or tell me a story about one of his clients. He'd pick up the broom and turn it into a microphone just to make me laugh.

I tried to tell myself that he only acted that way because he was relaxed, on holiday, and determined to make my two weeks the best they could be.

It was a lie though.

Harry had shown me who he was while we traveled, and I knew it was real.

He was the first thing on my mind when I woke each morning, which was really unnerving, especially when I'd turn to find a picture of Blake smiling at me.

I glanced down at the picture of Blake on my desk, my insides coiling as I lifted it up, kissed the glass, and popped it into my "take home" box. He was inside me; I didn't need a photo of him on my desk anymore.

I frowned at my rationale, then startled when my door clicked open.

"Sorry, did I surprise you?" Troy's voice was

deep and friendly, a soothing sound that could relax anyone. That's why he made such a good child counselor.

"No, that's fine. Come on in, Troy. How's it going?"

"Good." His smile was so broad it kind of dominated his large face. It matched perfectly with the rest of him. He was a tall, powerful man with soft, contradicting eyes. His taut muscles and bulky frame housed the kindest heart in the world. The kids he worked with adored and trusted him, and they had every right to.

Troy Baker was good to his core.

"So, what brings you into 7GB today?"

He smiled at the number and letters on my door, then ambled in. "I need to talk to you about one of the girls you'll be teaching this year—Brandy Hiseman." He passed me a manila file, and I flicked it open to see a beautiful girl with dark brown eyes and olive skin smiling up at me. I touched her photo, then skimmed the notes.

"Her parents are getting a divorce and it's turning ugly." Troy sighed, perching his butt on the edge of one of the desks. "Her mom wants to take her to Chile so she can be with her family, and the dad's fighting like a hellhound. Brandy's caught right in the middle of it. Now that she's twelve, she has a right to say where she'd like to go, and she's completely torn. She spent half the summer hiding in her room and the other half in my office." Troy scrubbed a hand over his face, looking tired and sad. "Anyway, she's going to be in your class."

I slapped the file closed and crossed my arms. "And why do you look so hesitant about that?"

He cringed, his sharp nose twitching as he looked to the floor. "Please don't take this the wrong way, but you were a robot last year. You were efficient, thorough, polite, and you didn't notice one of your students."

My jaw worked to the side as I absorbed his insult, knowing he was right. Flicking Brandy's file open again, I stared at the contents, but the ink blurred on the page. As much as I loved and admired Troy, I hated how observant he was.

"I tried to get her into Sharon's class, but she's already got a couple of special needs this year, and you were the next pick."

I cleared my throat, keeping my hazy eyes on the file.

"Jane..." Troy's soft voice forced me to look up at him. "This girl, Brandy, she really needs to be seen right now. She's feeling torn and frightened. The last thing she wants to do is come to school and face all her friends again. But she needs to be here. She needs to get out of that house and do something normal. And she really needs teachers who are going to support her through this process. It's going to be a hellish year."

I lifted my chin and looked him right in the eye. "I know all about those. I understand pain and loss, Troy. I know what it's like to feel ripped in half. So don't worry. I can be there for her. I can help her."

I finished with a pointed glare that made him

smile. His lips quirked up at the side, his pale eyes gleaming. "You seem brighter."

I grunted and got busy cleaning my already tidy desk. I moved the stapler from the right corner to my top drawer then realigned the notepad and pen holder.

He chuckled and walked across to me. "You know, this is good. I mean, you're showing real emotion. Last year you gave me nothing, but now I'm getting a whole lot of angst going on. Straightening up your desk with your shaky little fingers and that look on your face."

"Would you stop?" I slapped Brandy's file down and glared at him. "Don't look at my face."

I got a good view of his straight white teeth as he planted his feet and grinned at me. "What'd you do this summer?"

"I went away and tried to discover myself," I grumbled, rolling my eyes and willing myself not to open up about Harry.

Both Sarah and my mother had tried and failed to find out details. I basically left the gorgeous Brit out of my holiday retell. As far as my parents and best friend knew, I'd adventured around France, Spain, and Portugal all by myself...in a rented yellow Bambino. I only showed them photos of me on my own, moving all the Harry and Jane selfies into a separate folder so I could keep him a secret. I didn't even know why I was doing it. I guess I just wasn't ready to talk about him.

"So..." Troy wriggled his eyebrows, bringing me back to the present. "What'd you find?"

I bit my lips together, my throat too thick to respond. I wanted to tell Troy. He was a safe bet. He wasn't close to any of my friends; we knew a few people by association, but we only ever chatted in a work environment. The chances of him bumping into Sarah and then telling her what I said were slim to none.

Clearing my throat, I spit out the truth…sort of. "I discovered a girl desperate to live it up and have fun but who's petrified of feeling…anything." I ended in a whisper, but Troy heard me.

His gaze softened with compassion. "Feelings hurt."

I nodded. "But that can also be good. I mean, the good ones… They're amazing." My insides squeezed as I recaptured the waterfall moment and the crazy dancing in the restaurant.

I locked my jaw against them while Troy's smile grew bright and hopeful. "Wow. Jane, this is great progress. I'm so glad you felt something again."

"I don't know if I am or not," I grumbled.

"Who is he?"

I paused, wondering how he knew. I hadn't mentioned a guy.

But I was talking to Troy—the man could get anything out of anyone.

Picking a pen out of my holder, I rolled it in my hands, focusing on the spinning tip so I didn't have to look at the counselor. "You don't know him. A guy I met in England, and…" I shook my head and smiled. "It was crazy. We just went on this whirlwind vacation. Two complete strangers just having a blast together. I've never done something so out of character and I've never felt..."

My voice petered out.

I'd never felt that way before?

What about Blake?

My heart jerked and sputtered, making it hard to breathe.

"Sounds awesome." Troy's voice was so upbeat. "Can you figure out why you're feeling upset?"

A little lightheaded, I slumped into my seat and dropped my pen. It rolled to the edge of the desk, balancing precariously before tumbling over the side. Troy let it clatter to the floor. It stopped against his flip-flop, and then he bent down to pick it up. Placing it lightly in front of me, he gave me a knowing smile and waited for me to voice what he probably already knew.

"He whispered that he loved me when we were saying goodbye, and I just...bailed. Pretended I didn't hear him."

"What are you so afraid of?"

"Really?" I snapped. "You seriously don't know!"

His smile was calm and I sighed, recognizing his technique. It was up to me to voice my feelings.

"Blake's been my one and only. He was my soul mate, and I never thought I'd have feelings for another man. Maybe that was naive and overly romantic, I don't know!" I flicked my hands up. "But he's owned me for years. He was the keeper of my heart. How do I give it to someone else?"

Scratching his eyebrow, Troy leaned back

against the desk again, crossing his ankles and looking so damn relaxed, considering the turmoil going on inside of me. "You know, I've never felt that way about a woman before. I really hope I do one day, and until then I'm probably no authority on this kind of stuff. But I'm pretty sure I'm right when I say that the heart's an amazing thing. It's always bigger than we think it is, and it has this magical ability to keep expanding." Standing tall, he gave me one of his classic smiles, then turned for the door. "It all comes down to you and how big you're willing to let it grow." Stopping at the door, he glanced over his shoulder and winked at me. "If the Grinch can do it, I'm one hundred percent sure you can too."

I snickered and watched him leave, my erratic heart desperately trying to find its rhythm. Troy's words sank into me, working like a soft balm to take the heat from my fears and maybe help me believe that there was room enough for two.

TWELVE

HARRY

Jane left ten days ago and it didn't matter how hard I tried, I was bloody miserable without her. She was in my dreams at night. Memories haunted me while I worked. It didn't help that I couldn't stop playing "Every Little Thing She Does Is Magic." I'd become obsessed with the song. It fueled my memories of her, and I was trapped in this vicious cycle of torment.

Even buttering my toast for breakfast, I remembered how she liked to spread her jam all the way to the edges. It was like watching an artist paint, the way she'd glide the knife over her bread and get it just right. She'd then cut two perfect triangles, and I'd be mesmerized by her mouth as she ate. Thank God it'd been summer and I was able to hide behind a pair of dark shades.

Did she sense me watching her?

Did she know how much she'd really captured me?

I guessed not.

She hadn't tried to call or track me down, and I didn't feel right about pursuing her. I didn't want to be some kind of stalker.

We'd made a deal: *Adios. Thanks for a good time. Go our separate ways.*

No one warned me she'd linger after it was done.

But I guess I should have known better. Tammy was still nestled into a corner of my heart, wedged in tight and not going anywhere.

With a heavy sigh, I walked up Mum's front path and curved around the rose bushes. Since turning our house into a bed and breakfast, I'd gotten into the habit of using the back door. Guests would sometimes read in the living room, and I didn't like to stride through and disturb them.

As soon as I'd moved to London for design school, Mum had reformed our house. Dad had re-entered our lives by that stage. Mum refused to take him back, in spite of all his groveling, but they seemed to have found this weird kind of happiness between them. He lived a block away in a tiny studio apartment and spent most days at the house doing maintenance, garden work, and being the husband he should have been fifteen years ago.

I nudged the door open with my arm and was welcomed with the smell of roasting beef, frying onions, and Mum's mashed potatoes. Peas and carrots were boiling in the saucepan on the stove, and I had to give in to a little smile. I loved Mum's roasts.

"Darling." Mum turned from stirring the gravy, her round cheeks red from the heat. "How are you?"

"Good." I pecked her cheek, staying low so she could give me a proper kiss on my dimple.

She patted my cheek. "You need to shave."

"It's called stubble, Mum." I ran my fingers through my short bristles. "It makes me handsome."

"It makes you spiky and un-kissable."

I made a face behind her back, pulling a beer from the fridge as Dad wandered in.

"Hello, my boy. How was Spain?" He slapped my arm as he walked past, nicking the beer out of my hand. I rolled my eyes and opened the fridge for another one. It was actually the perfect excuse to avoid the question.

I'd told Nan everything, of course, but I didn't really want to dish it out to my parents. They wouldn't get it the same way Nan did.

I opened my beer and threw the cap at the rubbish bin. It bounced off the rim and landed near Mum's feet. With a sigh, I grabbed it and threw it away before Mum told me off.

"So, Spain good?"

Of course he didn't drop it.

"Yeah, Dad. Spain was great. Good weather. Great food. It was fun."

"Well, if you were that girl's tour guide, of course it was." Mum winked and smiled at me, her eyes skimming past Dad before returning to the gravy.

They shared a look I could easily interpret— worry for their youngest child. A boy named Harry who couldn't seem to find his way back into love.

I glared between them, but Mum just gave me a rosy smile and asked, "How's Nan?"

"Yeah, she's doing well." My voice was tight to match my smile.

"She missed you while you were away, but Renee popped over with the kids to entertain her." Mum paused, the way she always did before telling me something I needed to hear but probably didn't *want* to hear. "She did quite well without you, Harry."

Meaning: you're a grown man. Stop using your grandmother as an excuse not to join the world again.

I patted Mum on the shoulder and avoided responding by following Dad out of the kitchen.

"So, why am I meeting these guests for dinner?" I took a swig of my beer and perched on the arm of the sofa.

"They're old friends from when you were a kid. Renee remembers them. Anyway, they moved to London and are just down for a catch-up. Mum wanted a family dinner, so here we all are." I looked around the empty living room and Dad chuckled. "Here we all *will be*, if your sister ever gets here."

"Apparently having children makes you late to everything."

"Renee's been running late her whole life." Mum bustled in with a basket of freshly baked dinner rolls. "I should have told her to be here at six."

"It's all right, Mum. Dad and I can keep the guests happy while we wait."

"Well, that's good to hear!" a voice boomed from the stairwell, followed by a hearty laugh.

I stood and put on a smile, extending my hand when my father introduced me to Mr. and Mrs. Fairweather.

"Look at you. You're like a pine tree." She chortled, nudging her husband with her elbow. "I remember when you were this high with mud on your knees and a rip in your shirt. You were the scruffiest little munchkin."

"Yes, well not much has changed." Mum appeared again, winking at her friend, who immediately offered to help her in the kitchen.

I raised my bottle and asked Mr. Fairweather, "Can I get you a beer?"

"Let me do that." Dad disappeared, leaving me to chat with the older man on my own.

"So…" I tipped back on my heels. "Are you retired like Dad…or just on holiday?"

"Retired last year after a long and illustrious career at the American Embassy." He chuckled and shook his head. "Feels strange after working there for over twenty years. End of an era."

"The American Embassy?" I nearly choked out the words, my heart picking up pace as my brain computed what he'd just said.

"Yes, in Kensington."

"Twenty years?" I raised my eyebrows, hope flying through me like rockets.

"That's right."

"I don't suppose you, ah, ever worked with a...Mr. Buford?"

"Reggie Buford? Yes! I remember him well." The man grinned. "He left maybe eight, nine years ago, took his British wife and daughter back to America with him."

I swallowed, my heart pounding so hard I could barely ask the question. "I don't suppose you know where."

"Los Angeles, I think it was. Not sure if they're still there, but...he was a good man. We were sad to see him leave."

"Los Angeles," I repeated, no doubt sounding like a dumb fool.

"Yes." Mr. Fairweather nodded, his thick eyebrows dipping as he stared at my face. "You all right there, son? You're looking a little pale."

I jerked up straight and forced a happy grin. "No, I'm fine. Would you excuse me?"

Dad strode in as I ducked out of the room. Their conversation turned to white noise as I shakily yanked out my phone and started a search.

I told myself I wasn't going to do it, but meeting Mr. Fairweather was like a sign. I mean, fancy talking to a person who had actually worked with Jane's father. Surely the fates wanted us together. I mean, didn't they?

My phone had never worked so slowly as I waited for Safari to open. I started Googling *Jane Buford, LA* then quickly deleted the text and wrote *Georgiana Buford, LA*. The name was rare. I'd have a much better chance.

Nothing obvious popped.

There were a couple of Facebook pages with people who had names kind of similar but not quite the same. The surnames were different or the spelling wasn't right.

Spelling!

Jane said her name was spelled differently.

Holding my breath, I tried again with *Georjana Buford, LA.*

I got a hit.

One beautiful, glorious hit for a private school in Pasadena, LA—Strantham Academy. Following the Staff List link, I found a picture of Jane. Her red hair was combed back into a tight, neat ponytail, her green eyes were calm and emotionless, and she wasn't smiling. I recognized her, but I didn't.

I wondered if the photo was taken around the time of her non-marriage.

Browsing the website, I took a screenshot of the address before sliding the phone back into my pocket.

"We're here! Sorry we're late!" Renee burst through the door with her young tribe. "Oh, hello, Mr. Fairweather... Yes, I remember you. How nice to see you again."

I walked into the living room as she kissed the man on both cheeks.

"Uncle Harry!" my nephew shouted, jumping over his sister to reach me. I hoisted him up in the air and then got tackled around the legs by his twin brother. "Oi!" I laughed, stumbling back and taking the scuffle away from sweet little Emeline, who was sucking her thumb and clinging to her mother's skirt.

I tamed the boys relatively quickly, and they settled down after a barking order from their father.

"Sorry, Dad," they mumbled in unison before shuffling over to the toy box.

Their father kept his stern face on until they were past him, and then he winked at me and grinned. I laughed and patted my back pocket. My phone was still tucked safely inside. My heart warred with my head as I decided what to do about Jane.

My nephews got busy building a wooden train track in the corner. Emmi toddled over to them and sat down, picking up a train and sucking on the wooden wheel.

Renee's husband, Greg, leaned forward and whispered something in my sister's ear, pointing out the children. She turned and watched the boys build their track around Emmi while she made excited squeals and flapped her arms. Renee laughed and gazed up at her husband. They shared a little moment before he kissed her, and I was struck by the beauty of it all.

That was what Tammy had wanted—a marriage, a family, a life together.

I'd refused, and lost her because of it.

I didn't know exactly what Jane wanted, but as I stood there watching my sister's family, I started to figure out what *I* wanted.

Jane.

I wanted to be with Jane.

To see her smile, hear her laughter, dive into an in-depth conversation about art, history, movies, travel…*Star Wars*.

I wanted to dance with her again.

I wanted to kiss her.

And whether she'd appreciate me turning up on her doorstep or not, I knew it was the only way to do it. I *had* to see her again. I had to tell her, to her face, how much she meant to me and how I wasn't ready to let her go.

THIRTEEN

JANE

"Brandy, can I see you before you go, please?"

She huffed, her shoulders slumping forward as she let her peers pass her then headed over to my desk. I put on the kindest smile I could. I'd read her entire file, plus had another meeting with Troy. I hadn't met her parents, but I had a decent picture of what was going on, and I could imagine how hard it must be for her.

"So." I threaded my fingers together. "How's your first week been?"

She gave me a blank glare and pursed her lips.

I inwardly winced but somehow managed to

keep my smile intact. "Okay, look. I know you're going through a tough time right now and school is probably the last place you want to be, but it's safe here. And I just want you to know that if you need anything, I'm here for you. But I can't help you if you won't let me." I glanced to her desk, then put my stern voice on. "Drawing artwork on your desktop would usually score you at least one lunchtime detention. I'm going to let this one slide if you agree not to do it again. I don't want to send you to the principal's office after only three days at school."

She rolled her eyes, her pretty face dipping into a surly frown. "Fine. Whatever. Can I go now?"

I sighed. "Sure. Have a nice weekend."

"Like that'll happen." She gave me a cynical frown before stalking out of the room, her thick boots thumping on the floor.

Resting my butt against my desk, I gazed across the empty space and crossed my arms. The kids had started midweek, and the three days had gone by in a flurry of welcome activities and pre-assessments. I glanced over my shoulder at the pile of grading I had to do. I was teaching English to grades six and seven, plus had a homeroom to manage. Brandy was in my homeroom as well as my seventh-grade English class. I could already sense she was going to make my year a tough one.

So far, she'd done nothing more than graffiti her desk. I walked over to it and ran my fingers into the deep groves. There was no picture, just jerky lines and deep loops. With a sigh, I shuffled back to the front of the room.

My shoes sounded loud in the empty space. As soon as I reached my desk, I flicked on my music and rested my phone in the corner. The soft tune "Wherever You Go" played over me while I reached for the sixth-grade summer vacation recounts and started assessing.

As I read over their summer stories, my mind kept traveling back to Europe and my perfect summer. It had been the most amazing two weeks of my life. It felt wrong to think that. My best moments should have been when Blake was alive. I had so many happy memories with him.

But those two weeks in Europe…

My lips curled with a smile as I recaptured different moments with Harry…and his sweet smile and charming sense of humor. Those kind eyes. Those strong arms.

"I miss him," I whined, dropping my pen and wishing I'd had the courage to acknowledge what he'd whispered to me when we hugged goodbye.

But I shouldn't have missed him.

I couldn't pursue it.

It didn't make sense! We had two very separate lives. Long distance never worked. I just had to let him go and move on. At least he was alive. I wasn't mourning a loss, just missing a magical time in my life.

That was all.

Shuffle play selected "Wherever You Go" again as if it were trying to tell me something.

I grabbed my phone and went to skip it but then

changed my mind, suffering through the song and lamenting the fact Harry wouldn't be following me anywhere, because I ignored his sweet words and cut him off before anything more could develop.

He was probably getting on with his life, working hard and charming some other lucky lady with his sweet smile and adorable sense of humor...those hard abs and strong biceps...

Snatching the next recount off the pile, I scowled at the paper and forced myself to read it. I spent the next hour and a half trying to read, assess...and convince myself that I was right about Harry and our Europe utopia.

Needless to say, by the time I'd finished grading, I was in a foul mood and pretty much depressed. It was nearly five o'clock on a Friday afternoon, and all I had to look forward to was going home to an empty apartment and cooking a meal for one.

Then what?

A romantic chick-flick?

No, thank you.

But watching some awesome sci-fi wasn't going to make me feel better either. It'd just make me miss Harry all over again.

The list I'd started to motivate me out of my rut sat by my bed waiting for me to cross off some more, but I wasn't sure I could do it without Harry.

Pulling down the blinds, I did a final scan of my classroom before locking up and heading to the parking lot. I couldn't help thinking I was right back to square one, except now I had no engagement ring. I still sensed Blake with me, but was that more because I was willing him there? Desperately trying to cling to something that was passing?

So where did that leave me?

Alone again.

Blake-less.

Harry-less.

Joy-less.

I was worried I'd fall into robot mode again, and I could not let that happen. I couldn't do that to my students again, to my family and friends.

A dull headache started in the back of my brain as worries skittered through me. The hallways were vacant, making the clip of my heels echo off the empty walls. I was usually one of the last to leave, which never normally bothered me, but that day it just felt like another reminder of how lonely and pathetic I was.

Lifting my chin, I put on a brave face as I rounded the corner into the main entrance. If Principal Rogers still happened to be there, I didn't want him reading my mood. Instead, I was surprised to find Gabby still on reception.

"Oh, hi!" She nearly giggled. "I was just about to call you through the intercom."

"Hi." I gave her a confused frown. "You're working kind of late for a Friday." I leaned my arm against the counter while her round, merry face tinged red.

"Yes, well, the beginning of the school year can be a very busy time." Her gaze darted over my shoulder like she was trying to tell me something.

My eyebrows dipped into a V and I started to ask, "What were you going to call me ab...?" The words evaporated as I turned and spotted Harry standing in the waiting area. His hair was tousled, his whiskers a little longer than normal.

He flashed me that classic smile of his, showing off his slightly crooked front teeth and filling me with a sense of warmth I couldn't even start to deny.

"Hi," I whispered.

"Hi." He waved then tucked his hand into his pocket. "Jane." He said my name like it tasted sweet on his lips.

"What are you doing here?"

I knew. I mean, of course I knew, but it made sense to ask for some reason.

"I'm sorry to just show up like this." He swallowed, running a hand through his messy curls. "I'm not a stalker, I promise. It's just my dad knows a guy who knows your dad and we got chatting. LA came up and I thought, well, how many Georjana Buford's could there possibly be in LA? And there's one." He held up his finger. "Just one."

I think I stopped breathing for a moment. All I could do was gape at him.

He was there. I thought I'd never see him again...and he was standing right there.

"I know we said adios and we're supposed to go our separate ways, but the thing is, I can't stop thinking about you. And I just had to come and see you before I turned away for good. I just had to try…"

I pressed my lips together, emotions raging through me so thick and fast, it was a struggle to find the right words. Blinking a couple of times, I let out this weak, breathy laugh then sputtered, "You—you tracked me down and flew all the way here on the off-chance that I was lying when I pretended not to hear you say 'I think I'm in love with you'?"

His eyes narrowed as he caught up with what I'd just confessed.

"Right." I bobbed my head, still kind of dazed.

"Right." He repeated my squeak in a deep voice that sent tendrils of desire racing through my core. I glanced over my shoulder. Gabby was leaning in, listening to our every word with an excited grin.

If I wasn't careful, the staffroom on Monday was going to be a hotbed of gossip.

I gave her a weak smile, already knowing I was too late to stop that from happening. But she didn't have to see everything.

I transferred my weak grin to Harry, who gave me a doubtful frown.

"So…am I keeping the backpack on or slipping it off to hug you?"

I swallowed and dipped my head. "Keep it on."

When I looked back up, his sad eyes nearly tore my heart out.

I quickly stammered, "But…f-follow me."

Tipping my head back toward my classroom, I left Gabby behind. She wouldn't be ballsy enough to follow us, and I didn't want her watching me hug Harry either. I couldn't wait to wrap my arms around him, which was why I was walking him back to my classroom rather than leading him to my car. My apartment was a half-hour drive away, and in rush hour, I wouldn't be able to feel his arms around me until after six.

I couldn't wait that long.

He didn't say anything as he followed me down the deserted hallways. I walked quickly, my heels sounding like machine gun fire. His sneakers squeaked on the tiles behind me.

With trembling fingers I unlocked my door and held it open for him. He gave me another sad, uncertain smile as he walked into the room.

I shut the door and locked it before turning to watch him scan my classroom. With the blinds down, the light was dim, but I didn't want to switch on the lights and alert anyone to our presence. Morris, the janitor, would have done his final lock-up round already, but still. He probably wouldn't have left the school yet.

"Um..." My heart thundered as I tucked my bangs behind my ear and slowly approached him. "Sorry about that. The school secretary, bless her, is a total gossip and I just didn't want her to..."

Harry turned to face me and my words dried up.

I couldn't believe he was there. He'd come all that way because he couldn't stop thinking about me.

The thought made a smile grow on my lips.

Nerves made me bite at it and scratch the side of neck. Harry's gaze drank me in as he slowly slid the pack off his shoulders.

It thumped onto the floor and jolted me into action.

I surged across the room, grabbing his face and kissing him with everything I had. His strong arms encircled my waist, lifting me off my feet as his tongue lashed against mine. Our kisses were hungry and loud as whatever pent-up passion we'd had locked within us could no longer be contained.

He lowered me to my feet, his hand traveling up my back and holding the nape of my neck. I deepened the kiss even more—somehow it was possible—yet I still couldn't kiss him hard enough. He moaned into my mouth, igniting the dormant embers within me. They sparked and flamed as I tugged at his shirt.

"I've missed you too," I murmured between desperate kisses, yanking off his shirt and throwing it onto the ground. Running my hands up his naked chest, I kissed his pecs, then lightly sucked all the way up to his shoulders. "I couldn't stop thinking about you."

"All the time," he puffed, flicking up the bottom of my summer dress and palming my thigh. "It was crazy."

I giggled into his mouth. "Perfect for us, then."

His laughter hit my neck, sending my senses into overdrive as he kissed the tender skin. He lifted me off the floor and spun me around so I could sit on my desk. This was when being a neat-freak came in handy. My desk was basically bare, allowing plenty of room for sexy little trysts. Not that I'd ever had one on my desk.

Giddy excitement made me smile as I wrapped my legs around his hips and my breasts squished against his rock-hard chest.

I was already pulsing with desire, but it skyrocketed the second my wet cotton briefs brushed against his erection.

Common sense left me for good at that point.

I completely forgot that I was in my classroom. It didn't even occur to me that having sex on my desk wasn't the most natural thing in the world. My frantic hands went for his trousers, unbuttoning them and yanking them down. His impressive manhood, so hard yet smooth, brushed against my thigh, and I nearly came on the spot.

It'd been over a year since I'd had sex, and Harry's touch ignited me.

"Please tell me you have protection," I whimpered into his mouth.

Pulling away from me, he bent down and dug into the pants around his ankles, rising with a foil-wrapped square and a triumphant smile.

"I was being optimistic."

I laughed and snatched it off him, unwrapping it with my teeth and sliding it on. His breaths were heavy in my ear, sending even more sparks flying through me. The second he was wrapped, his lips hit mine again. The kiss was the most intense yet, his hot tongue plunging into my mouth as he held my head with a trembling hand.

I raised my hips, bumping against him with an urgent need that was borderline embarrassing. He snickered and pulled back, removing my underwear with a painful slowness. His eyes were on mine as he flicked the panties off my ankle and dropped them to the floor. Lightly brushing my skin with the backs of his fingers, he drew a line from my knees to my center. His hazel eyes were bright with desire as he ran his fingers around my opening then plunged inside.

My head flopped back and I let out a moaning kind of gasp as I gripped his arm to keep myself from falling. He leaned me back, gently sucking my neck and sending me to a new plane of pleasure. My pencil holder and stapler hit the floor with a bang but I didn't even flinch, too busy whimpering and mewling as my body took flight. Slipping his fingers out of me, Harry trailed his hand down my thigh before he hooked it under my knee and gave me what I'd been craving.

I cried out as he pushed into me.

His broad length owned me, filling me to my very core, stealing my breath and making me dizzy. It was impossible to stay quiet as he thrust in and out. His fingers dug into my thighs when I pulled my legs up, giving him easier access. He groaned and clenched my butt, thrusting harder and faster.

Our sexy song changed as we built to climax together. My whimpering moans blended with his, increasing in volume and intensity until we both let out a final shout. Harry leaned over me, gripping my shoulder as he jerked inside me a few more times.

Floating down from the high was nearly ethereal. I felt weightless as I blinked my fuzzy eyes and returned to earth. My limbs were limp and useless, my thighs slapping onto my desk as he moved away from me and cleaned himself up.

With shaky, puffy breaths, I slowly slid off the desk to retrieve my underwear. I nearly fell over trying to pull them back on, but Harry caught me against him, wrapping his arms around me and lifting me onto his knee as we toppled into my chair.

"Well, that was some hug." He smiled. "I must drop in to say hello more often."

Heat radiated from my skin and I rested my forehead into the crook of his neck while he laughed.

"What just happened?" I whispered.

I could feel his Adam's apple move as he swallowed and gently placed his hand on my thigh. "What we obviously both wanted." He kissed my forehead. "I came here with no expectations but, Jane, if you'll let me love you…"

I popped up to look into his eyes. Resting my hand on his cheek, I brushed my thumb over his stubble and nodded.

His smile was like a beacon, lighting up my dim classroom and filling me with unchecked joy. We just sat there grinning at each other like teenagers who'd just discovered the wonders of sex.

Finally Harry cleared his throat and patted my thigh. "Now, as much as I love your classroom, I don't suppose you have somewhere else I could stay tonight?"

I snickered and bit my lips together. My head bobbed erratically, shooing away the nervous energy pumping through me. He was spending the night at my apartment...in my bed. Not even the quiet murmurs of uncertainty firing through the back of my mind could stop that.

FOURTEEN

HARRY

My eyes popped open and I sniffed in a breath. The chair with my clothes draping over it was highlighted by the morning sun. The crack in the curtains allowed a perfect beam of yellow to shine across the wooden floors.

Rubbing a hand over my weary face, I rolled over the rumpled bed and looked through the sheer curtain to spy Jane standing in front of the stove. She was wearing nothing but a baggy T-shirt. I could just spy the curve of her butt beneath the cotton hem.

Bacon sizzled in the fry pan she was holding,

125

and the smell of brewing coffee, plus the stunning view, helped rouse me completely.

Quietly shuffling to the edge of the bed, I slid beneath the four-post curtain then tiptoed across to the guitar I'd spotted the night before. I wasn't the world's best player, but I was good enough to strum out a tune, and I thought it'd be the best way for Jane and me to start our first full day together.

Romance was the perfect way to a girl's heart, right?

We hadn't talked much the night before—too busy exploring each other's bodies—and I was looking forward to spending the day with her. Reliving a little of what we had in Europe. I didn't want to waste a second of my limited time.

I had just over a month until I had to return for Nan's ninetieth birthday. I couldn't get out of it. It would be the first time in years that her entire family would be together, and I had to be there.

Not wanting to let anyone down, I promised Mum I'd show, and then asked her to drive me to the airport.

At that stage, I still hadn't known if Jane would accept me or not. And I still didn't know if she'd be okay with me living with her for several weeks. We had so much to talk about, but all I could focus on was the fact she'd let me stay at all.

A huge grin dominated my face as I thought about her ready acceptance in the classroom.

Quietly lifting the guitar from its perch against the wall, I nestled it across my chest and wandered into the room, strumming the opening riff to

"Every Little Thing She Does Is Magic."

I barely made it through the first line of the first verse when she whipped around to face me, her green eyes bulging at the sight of me in tartan boxer shorts, playing her a love song.

"What are you doing?" she snapped.

Her sharp tone made me falter and my voice broke over the second line.

Sucking in a breath, she closed her eyes and made a fist as if fighting for control. "Can you put that down, please?"

Her tight voice made me frown, and I slowly lowered the guitar.

Storming toward me, she avoided eye contact while plucking the instrument from my hands and carefully placing it back.

I ran my fingers over the dining chair and smiled at her when she returned to the stove top. "I didn't realize my singing was that bad."

She snickered and scratched her forehead with shaky fingers. "Sorry, I just..." She picked up the tongs then swallowed and laid it down. Turning off the gas, she slowly turned to face me. Her lips pushed into a sad smile, and she still wouldn't look me in the eye when she murmured, "That guitar is very precious and no one ever touches it."

"Okay." I nodded, desperate to ease the tension radiating off her.

Her cheeks began to tinge red as she gripped the counter behind her and looked to the floor.

"Who did it belong to?"

"I..." Her expression crumpled, so I filled in the

gap for her.

"Ah, the guy who broke your heart."

Her fragile expression morphed to anger. It flashed across her face, her green glare dark as it hit me in the chest.

I inched away from it, wondering what had happened to our night before. The carefree laughter, the all-consuming passion. I'd expected to wake up to a lighthearted Jane, not what was facing me.

Wishing I was wearing pants so I could slide my hands into my pockets, I had to suffice with crossing my arms. Forcing a soft smile, I used the calmest tone I could, hoping to coax the truth from her.

"I can see how much it still hurts you, so why do you keep it?"

Her eyes glassed with tears, her anger making way for a deep sorrow. I recognized the emotion on her face. I'd felt it myself, and it made me start to question my assumptions that the guy had simply ditched her.

With a soft sniff, she slashed a finger under her eye. "To remember the good times, I guess. Sometimes when I wake in the morning, I roll over and see it there and I remember a moment. One of the good ones before everything turned to shit."

I got it.

I completely understood.

That was why I kept my photo of Tammy...and all her beloved books. Each morning when I gazed across my room to her little bookshelf, it did one of two things: filled me with despair...or gave me a moment. Those were the days I lived for—those sweet memories that filled me with bittersweet nostalgia.

"Sorry," Jane mumbled. "I don't want to ruin the morning. I'm always melancholy when I'm over-tired."

I gave her one of my rare blushing grins as I relived the reason for our exhaustion. Her cheeks flamed red, hiding all her freckles. She spun away from me and grabbed the toast out of the machine. Flicking the lid off the butter, she started to spread it to the edges—her perfect buttering routine.

A soft smile lit my lips as I watched her hands.

Noticing my phone on the table, I picked it up and found The Police's version of "Every Little Thing She Does Is Magic." Jane stilled as the music filtered into the room.

She wouldn't turn to face me, so I slowly approached her. "This song will forever make me think of you." Stopping behind her, I gently flicked the hair off her neck then placed my lips into the crook. "You're magic to me, Jane, and all I want to do while I'm here is give you good memories that you can wake up to."

Her shoulders relaxed and she pushed back against me, leaning her head on my shoulder so I could nip the end of her nose with my lips.

"I didn't mean to upset you. I'm sorry."

She reached behind her, teasing the curls at the nape of my neck with her elegant fingers. "You didn't. I shouldn't be so sensitive."

"You're allowed to have your treasured things. And I promise, I won't touch it again."

Her eyes warmed with affection, and she returned to buttering our toast. I bent down to rest my chin on her shoulder, my hands finding their way beneath her shirt. With a mind of their own, they traveled to her breasts, cupping them then giving them a gentle squeeze.

A husky moan escaped her, and she thrust her butt back into my growing erection.

"Give me a sweet memory now, Harry," she whispered, tugging at my boxers.

I massaged her breasts a little harder, running my tongue from her shoulder to her ear. Sucking her lobe into my mouth, I pinched her nipples, rolling them between my fingers until her knife clattered to the bench top.

She gripped the edge, pressing her bottom back against me again.

I dropped my shorts in one swift move, my erection nestling between her butt cheeks while I reached for the box of condoms at the end of the counter. It was a stretch, and we both ended up snickering as I tried to claim them without losing my position.

Wrestling one free, I tore it open with my teeth and quickly wrapped myself before scrambling beneath her shirt again. Her nipples were still erect, and I teased them until she was panting and quivering beneath my touch.

Spreading her legs, she rose to her tiptoes and leaned forward, pushing against me and silently telling me to get on with it. I obliged with a smile and she gasped as I slid home, my mind going fuzzy. Gliding my hand down her body, I thrust into her with a grunt, determined to make this her best memory ever. It didn't take me long to find her sweet spot, and I was soon stroking her with my finger as well. She let out a cute, whimpering moan as I teased her, rushing her to orgasm while I continued to plunge in and out of her.

The plate of toast slipped into the sink as she slapped her hand on the counter and started letting out these sexy cries. They fired through me, charging me to an intense, explosive finish. Grabbing her hips, I thrust in deep and hard, holding her tight while we shook against each other.

I wanted to say something charming and funny, but I couldn't speak past my thundering heartbeat. All I could do was lean forward and wrap my arms around her, gluing our bodies together. I kissed the back of her head then pressed my cheek against her luscious hair, inhaling her citrus scent and knowing that I'd found my new home.

FIFTEEN

JANE

I nibbled the edge of my toast, unable to wipe the smile from my face. I kept biting my lips together, hoping it would help, but it didn't work.

"On Top Of The World" was whistling through my apartment, a happy, sweet tune to match my insides.

Unchecked joy.

I could cross it off my list.

In spite of my early morning doubts, Harry had once again brought me to a place of complete surrender...and I wanted to surrender to him over and over again.

I hadn't realized how much I'd missed sex. Waking up beside someone, having someone send you over the edge like that...having someone to talk to...or stare at across the table.

I'd missed it.

Brushing the crumbs from his fingertips, Harry grinned at my hungry eyes. We hadn't said much to each other since he took me against my kitchen counter. My body was still buzzing from his magic touch, and he seemed unusually quiet. Although the goofy, dreamlike expression on his face told me he was feeling pretty much the same way I was.

Swallowing down his mouthful, he finished his coffee and then broke our silence. "So, what do you want to do today?"

My eyebrow peaked and I looked over at the kitchen counter. "What we did about twenty minutes ago." I leaned forward, drawing out my words nice and slowly. "All. Day. Long."

His eyes danced before he let out a growl and leaped from his chair. I squealed and laughed as he scooped me out of my seat and threw me over his shoulder. Tickling my bare butt, he carried me back to the bed, wrestling the curtain out of the way before flopping me onto the soft mattress and diving on top of me.

My belly bunched with laughter as he covered me with kisses, and we spent the rest of that Saturday making love, sleeping in each other's arms, and doing everything we'd wanted to do on our trip but did not have the courage to.

*****

Resting my head on Harry's chest, I traced invisible drawings on his torso while we lay there listening to music. His phone had been going all day, keeping us company as we orgasmed, slept, showered, and then got dirty all over again.

My body was blissfully sore.

Brushing my foot up his bare leg, I kissed his chest. I was too tired to talk or do anything more than just soak in his presence.

His strong body was comforting, like a rock I could lean against.

"Fireflies" started playing, the magical opening so familiar.

It made me think of the night we sat under the stars in Barcelona. We'd been on the beach staring up at the vast night sky. The air had cooled our sun-kissed skin, and I'd felt the kind of peace I'd been seeking ever since Blake died.

It'd wrapped itself around me, gifting me a moment.

Harry's arm had been pressed against mine as we marveled at the constellations, the twinkling diamonds decorating the inky black sky.

"Where were we the night we sat under the stars and tried to name the constellations?" The tips of Harry's fingers brushed up and down my arm, his husky voice warming my insides.

I smiled. "Barcelona."

"Well done." He kissed my hair. "This song always makes me think of that. The stars were like—"

"Fireflies," I finished for him, propping my chin on his chest and looking up at him. "I was thinking the same thing."

He tucked my bangs behind my ear and smiled at me. It was the kind of gaze that told me he loved me. "I've always loved that about us."

"What?" I whispered.

"That we think the same. Being with you is just so easy, Janey. It's like we were meant to be together."

I couldn't respond to that. I'd thought Blake was my soul mate, so how could I be meant for Harry? It didn't make sense in my head, despite what my heart was trying to tell me.

I was afraid to think about where this was going...what would become of Harry and me. He loved me. I could see it in his eyes. And I thought I loved him too, which only confused me. My heart was so full of Blake, yet I was trying to let another man in.

A good man.

A man who could make me happy.

But what if I lost him too?

Fear made my eyes glass with tears. Harry's expression dropped and he rolled over with a worried frown, cradling my head in the crook of his elbow.

"What is it?"

I couldn't tell him. I still didn't want to bring Blake into the room. It felt too weird and like maybe I was somehow betraying him.

Instead I shook my head and attempted a smile.

"Nothing," I whispered.

Running my nails through Harry's stubble, I focused on the scratchy sound, hiding my secrets by continuing the "Where Were We" game.

I pursed my lips then smiled. "Where were we when you had ice cream plastered all over the front of your shirt?"

Harry started laughing, and I soaked in his gorgeous face.

The only way to do this thing with Harry was to live in each moment. I couldn't think ahead to him leaving me, which he'd eventually have to do, and I couldn't think back to a point before I met him. All I could focus on was the fact that he was in LA, and for the next six weeks, he was mine.

SIXTEEN

HARRY

We spent the weekend in bed aside from Sunday afternoon when we did some grocery shopping. Our clothes were on the floor as soon as we'd finished unpacking the refrigerated goods.

Jane left for work on Monday morning, and I opened my laptop and cracked on with it. The week ticked by in a happy kind of rhythm that was both comfortable and exciting.

Working in her apartment felt much like working at Nan's house. I blasted my music, drowned in a sea of websites, and was the happiest I'd been in years.

Yeah, even happier than when I'd been with Tammy. I loved that woman with all my heart, but I couldn't give her what she wanted, and it made our little house a tense place some days. I had every excuse in the world—we're too young to get married, there's nothing wrong with living together, marriage doesn't last, why taint what we have with wedding rings?

I'd been a self-centered, scared fool.

It wasn't until she was gone that I realized that marriage wouldn't have changed what we'd had. If anything, it would have made it better, because Tammy would have been happy. I'd loved her like a husband loved a wife. I just hadn't wanted to label it that way. Just because her parents had been happily wed didn't mean mine had.

Rubbing my forehead, I pushed thoughts of my dad aside and squinted at the screen. A mild headache was kicking in. Jane's dining room table wasn't exactly set up ergonomically like my place was. I'd have to be careful and monitor my neck and shoulder pain.

I stood tall and did a few stretches, then checked the time. Jane would be finishing work in a couple of hours. The last few nights, she'd stayed after the final bell to do marking then wandered in the door around five thirty, pretty exhausted. I'd cooked dinner for her and massaged her feet, listened to her talk about a problem girl in her class and the stress over trying to help her. I could do it again if she needed me to, but I thought it was about time we had a little fun.

Closing my laptop, I spun on my heel and started searching her apartment for the Life List. I wouldn't have been surprised if she hadn't added to it once since leaving England. That would not do. It was a list night; I could feel it in my bones.

Rummaging through her drawers—yes, it felt a little weird, but I hoped she'd understand that my intentions were pure—I came across a framed photo of Jane with her arms wrapped around a handsome-looking guy with shoulder-length hair. He was grinning at the camera while she smiled up at him. A green emerald glinted on her ring finger. Scowling at the image, I threw it back in the drawer. What kind of idiot turned his back on a girl like Jane? I didn't know what happened to him, but the fact he wasn't around told me how blind he must have been.

I crossed to her nightstand and glanced at the guitar against the wall. Maybe I was wrong. You didn't treasure an object like that unless the person you'd loved was gone for good.

My insides twisted into a tight, sickening knot, fueling my determination to give Jane another night of happiness. Lifting the stack of books beside her phone charger, I unearthed the list. It swooped to the floor and landed against my foot.

"There you are."

I noticed that she hadn't added anything new, although *unchecked joy* had been crossed off. I didn't remember what that one was.

Uncapping the first pen I could find, I laid the paper flat and added another thing to the list. I then folded the sheet and slid it into my back pocket.

It took me ten more minutes and two phone calls to get myself ready, and then I was out the door. I was giddy with triumph by the time I pulled the rental car into the Strantham Academy lot. Students were dribbling out the doorway as they made their way to the bus, the waiting cars, or the walk home.

I bustled through the traffic, the only fish swimming upstream. By the time I reached Jane's classroom, the student body had thinned to a trickle and I was able to hop around a little guy with a big mouth and his basketball-bouncing friend.

Jane's voice reached me before I saw her. I slowed my steps and listened in.

"Brandy, I'm really happy that you're no longer destroying school property, but you can't spend the rest of this year doodling on a notepad. I need some work out of you, sweetie."

Her kind words were met with a disgruntled huff.

My forehead wrinkled, and I softly stepped into the doorway so I could see what this Brandy looked like. She was short with long, dark locks that reached nearly to her hips. Her face was round, her skin olive, and she had these brown, haunted eyes that made my heart squeeze with sympathy. You didn't have to hear her speak to know she was a lost kid, hiding her hurt behind a fragile wall of anger. I knew. I used to be just like her.

Jane bit her lips together, obviously striving for calm. "Listen, I know things are difficult right now. I know you're sick of hearing me say that. But, come on, wasting your time here? You're only hurting yourself. And failing school will not help you achieve whatever it is you're trying to achieve. All I'm asking for is a little effort. Show me what you're capable of."

"I don't care about school. I don't want to put in any effort, don't you get that?"

"Well, what do you care about?"

"Nothing!" Her voice pitched high, the anguish on her face making my heart bleed.

I stepped into the room, alerting them both to my presence. I wanted to grin and wink at Jane's surprise, but I kept my eyes trained on Brandy. Giving her a kind smile, I wagged my finger at her and said, "Now, I don't know if that's true."

SEVENTEEN

JANE

Brandy's lip curled as my heart started pounding. What was Harry doing? I had to tread carefully with this girl. I couldn't have him making things worse.

I ran my hand across my throat, silently telling him to stop, but he ignored me, sliding his hands into his pockets and giving Brandy a charming smile.

"I don't know anyone who cares about nothing."

Brandy scoffed and rolled her eyes. "Whatever, man."

Her gaze then shot to me, and she gave me a quick *who the hell is this guy* kind of look. But then he started talking again, stealing her attention with a gentle confession.

"You know, I was eight when my dad took off. No word, no note, just left us high and dry. Mum was forced back to work so she could support us, and then she had this mental breakdown. My nan had to come and take care of us. It was a really shit time."

My eyes bulged as he swore in front of my student, but it was kind of fitting. My heart ached for him as I pictured little eight-year-old Harry trying to work it all out.

"I don't remember everything, but I do remember being filled with this constant rage. I just wanted to find my dad and beat the living crap out of him."

Brandy snickered, the edge of her mouth curling into a rare smile.

"I mean, I guess I still loved him and all that, but I was hurt and Mum was depressed and my family just was falling apart."

"So, what'd you do?" Brandy asked.

"Well, I tried beating the crap out of one of the kids at school instead."

"You get in trouble?"

"Yeah, suspended and then grounded for like a month. But it was good."

"Good?" Brandy gave him a skeptical frown.

"Yeah, well, being stuck up in my room gave me time to get it out. At first I tried punching pillows, but it wasn't that satisfying. I wanted to see Dad's face when I told him what a loser he was. Then I'd punch him and watch him bleed."

I swallowed, my throat swelling with emotion as I saw a flash of the little boy he once was.

"So, I decided to draw it. I drew picture after picture of me beating my dad down, telling him everything he'd done to our family. I made them like comic strips and told the story the way I wanted it done."

Brandy had gone still, her narrow glare giving way to open interest. "You draw?"

"Yeah." Harry grinned.

"You any good at it?"

He scratched the side of his nose, his smile humble. "My mum thinks so."

Brandy gave him a skeptical, *you're pathetic* kind of frown, which only made him laugh. Pulling out his phone, he showed her some of the artwork he'd shown me in Europe. Stuff he'd drawn and designed for his job, plus a few images of his niece and nephews. They were done in the Marvel Comics kind of style.

Brandy leaned across to look more closely at the phone, her eyebrows rising. "You did that?"

"Yeah. Bet it's not as good as yours though." Harry slid his phone away and lifted his chin at her bag. "Come on, give us a look."

Biting the edge of her lip, she unzipped her bag and pulled out a notepad, one I hadn't seen before. Harry flipped open the cardboard cover and gazed down at the first image. His face rose with a smile that told me he recognized whatever emotion Brandy had put on the page. Bobbing his head, he kept looking through, his voice rich with praise.

"These are really good."

Her lips twitched with a smile, showing off a small dimple on her left cheek.

Slapping the notepad shut, Harry passed it back and crossed his arms. "Tell you what, my little artist. Scratch your homework for tonight. Probably boring as hell anyway. Instead, I want you to draw whatever it is that's going in there." He pointed to her head. "And there." He pointed to her heart. "You get it out and onto paper. Trust me, it works." He winked and she gave him a full-blown smile—dimples and white teeth included.

Turning back to me with an awed grin, she shoved her notepad back into her bag and zipped it closed. "Is that cool with you, Miss B?"

I smiled. "Yeah, that's cool with me. And I'll make sure it's cool with your other teachers too."

Her eyes shone with gratitude, and then she waved and walked out of the room.

All I could do was blink at her as she disappeared into the hallway.

"How did you do that?" I nearly laughed, stepping across to Harry and wrapping my arms around his neck. "She smiled! A real smile!"

I pulled away from him and grinned at the bashful smirk on his face. "She just needs to tap into something that inspires her. As soon as I heard you say doodling, I felt like I was looking at a younger version of myself."

"I never knew that about your dad. I'm sorry."

Harry shrugged. "It's okay. Mum found her way, and then Dad came back. She refused to take him into her home again, but they've got this weird kind of friendship going on now."

"Why'd he leave?"

"Midlife crisis. It took him nearly five years to figure that out, and then another three to win us all over. Persistence pays, I suppose."

"That must have been a really tough time for you guys. I never knew."

"Yeah, well, there's a lot we don't know about each other, Janey." He ran a finger down my face, silently asking for something from me.

I gave him a hesitant smile and backed out of the embrace. "So, tell me why I have the pleasure of your company a few hours early today."

"Well…" He pulled a sheet of paper out of his pocket. "I hope you don't mind, but I found your list beside the bed and thought it was about time we added something new."

Taking the sheet off him, I glanced at the bottom and read: *go for a sexy drive to watch the sunset.*

I nodded, my eyebrows rising as I laughed. "What's a sexy drive?"

Pulling the keys out of his pocket, he jiggled them in the air. "I can tell you right now, it's not a Bambino, so just calm down."

I snorted and covered my mouth, my shoulders already shaking with laughter.

"Come on. Let me show you." He gathered up my bag and waited for me to slide my computer into the back pouch before carrying it outside for me. "But, seriously, before you get too excited, I know a motorbike would have been the coolest, sexiest thing I could find, but I'm not a huge fan."

I gripped his arm, hiding my emotion behind a smile. "Me neither."

"Good."

We strolled through the main entrance. Harry made Gabby blush with a wink and a smile. She gave me a double thumbs-up as I walked out of school earlier than I ever had before.

"Okay, close your eyes." Harry stepped behind me, covering my eyes with his hand.

We shuffled forward together, his long body guiding me. I'd never enjoyed walking blind. Surprises weren't my forte, but Harry's excitement was stirring mine, and by the time we stopped I was nearly giddy.

Opening my eyes, I let out a little squeal and jumped on the spot as I took in the red Corvette convertible. Harry was right. That beautiful machine screamed sexy.

"Can I drive?"

"Of course you can." He threw me the keys and walked me around to the driver's side. Acting like the gentleman he was, he opened the door for me, then ambled to the other side and vaulted in without opening his door.

"All right, my sexy little redhead. Take me somewhere magical." He pointed at me. "And your apartment doesn't count. I mean somewhere *else* magic."

I started the engine and gave him a sexy wink. "It's not the apartment that's magical, Harry. It's you and me."

His smile shone, lighting my way as I pulled out of the parking lot and headed for Malibu. I knew just the place to watch the sunset and maybe create a little more magic in the backseat of the convertible.

EIGHTEEN

HARRY

I'd been living with Jane for just over a week and was thoroughly in love with it. I hated that I had to leave her again, but I couldn't miss Nan's birthday.

"We don't know how many she has left. You, of all people, know the importance of making the most of these special moments, Harry."

Mum's reminder had turned my insides to mud. I'd already promised her I'd be there, but she obviously felt the need to really drive it home. She must have sensed how happy I was with Jane and started to worry I'd change my mind.

She had probable cause, I suppose. Being with Jane was everything I'd hoped it would be...and more.

Running a hand down my face, I tried to shake off the imminent dread of leaving her. What if something happened to her when I was gone?

It may have seemed like an over-the-top fear, but it was a niggle that lived inside me constantly. No one ever knew how much time they really had with someone, and I wanted to make the most of every second I could get with Jane.

I'd only be gone for a short time, but I had to be careful about my travel expenses. Living in LA wasn't exactly cheap, and it didn't help that I wanted to continually surprise Jane with expensive rental cars and nice dinners. She deserved it, and I wanted to be the guy to make her happy. But I wasn't exactly rolling in cash, and I'd have to save to be able to afford to return after Nan's birthday. And then when I did return, I'd only have a few months left until my visa ran out. I'd be forced back to England for a stint, unable to return until I met visa requirements again.

Was that what it would be like? Constantly having to say goodbye?

"Stop thinking so far ahead, you idiot," I muttered, tapping the space bar and bringing my screen back to life.

If I wanted to earn enough money to come back at all, I couldn't sit around pondering my fate. Squinting at the screen, I reread the job description and got to work on interpreting what the client wanted. By the end of the day, I'd managed to mock up something rather classy. I was about to email it to them with a triumphant little smirk when a key went into the lock.

My insides jumped with pleasant surprise…and a little confusion.

Jane had told me she'd have to stay late and catch up on some work.

"I can't work with you here. You're too distracting. I'll just do a late night at school."

I didn't love that idea, but she was right. It was kind of hard to stay away from each other. I planned on working late too.

"Well, she hasn't returned any of my calls, what am I supposed to do?" A female voice I didn't recognize wafted through the crack in the door as it started to open. "She gave me a key for a reason, Justin. She won't mind."

I froze at the table, my eyes glued to the door as a couple who looked to be around my age walked in—a slender blonde with sparkly blue eyes and a guy with dark curly hair.

They both jerked to a stop when they noticed me, and all I could do was raise my hand and smile. "Hi. Uh, hello."

They stood there for a moment, gaping at me, then looked at each other before frowning in unison and aiming two dark glares in my direction.

"W-who the hell are you?" the guy practically growled at me.

"Uh, I'm Harry." I stood from the table and wiped my hand on my jeans before extending it to introduce myself. "Harry Tindal."

The blonde continued to glare at me, crossing her arms and snapping, "What are doing in this apartment?"

"I'm staying here." I pointed behind me, at the bed of all things. Granted, a thoughtless move.

The woman's eyes bulged, her already milky skin paling further. "Who are you!" she yelled, flicking her hands in the air.

"I'm, um, well, I guess you could say I'm Jane's boyfriend?"

"Her boyfriend?" the girl mimicked me. "Jane doesn't have a boyfriend."

"I beg to differ." I pointed at the horrified couple and let out a breathy laugh that was killed by their unimpressed scowls. "She's working late tonight and I promised not to disturb her, but I could give her a call if you like, straighten this out?"

I turned to reach for my phone, but the blonde stopped me with a snap of her fingers. "Don't move. I'll call her."

Slipping my hands into my pockets, I tried to give the guy a friendly smile as the woman yanked her phone out of her bag and called Jane.

No dice.

He wasn't having any of it.

I had no idea who these people were. Jane had mentioned a few friends, but we never got specific. No histories...never thought it would cause any kind of complications, but there they were in dark curls and blonde waves. Staring me down and making me feel like the world's worst imposter.

NINETEEN

JANE

The phone in my bag started ringing. I'd slipped it away so I couldn't see it and be tempted to call Harry. I glanced down at my bag and wondered whether to ignore it.

But then he had promised not to call, so there was a good chance it wasn't him...which probably meant it was my mother. I'd had a breezy conversation with her two days ago, telling her I couldn't catch up for dinner on the weekend.

"You're a busy girl this year, darling."

"I'm just trying to make up for my bad start last year. Give me a few weeks and I'll make myself

available."

I'd need the company after Harry left anyway.

I sighed and ignored the call, figuring I'd phone back on my way home.

Leaning toward my computer screen, I continued planning out my lessons for the following week when my phone started buzzing again.

I tipped my head to the ceiling. "Oh, come on."

With a little huff, I pulled out my phone and noted Sarah's number on the screen.

"Frick," I muttered. I hadn't spoken to my best friend since Harry arrived. If anyone was going to get the truth out of me, it'd be her, and for some reason, I didn't want her knowing.

I didn't understand why.

Maybe because she was married to Blake's brother, or maybe because the four of us used to be inseparable and it felt weird bringing a new person into the mix. Whatever it was, I'd been avoiding her, and she'd obviously had enough.

Biting my lips together, I rubbed my thumb down the side of my phone, seriously considering ignoring her, but I didn't want her to worry.

I held my breath and answered, making sure a smile was in place by the time the phone was pressed against my ear.

"Hey, Sparky. How's it going?"

"There's a man in your apartment. He says he's your boyfriend. You have about thirty seconds to verify this or I'm calling the cops."

I nearly dropped the phone. My heart jumped

into my throat and started hammering, making it really hard to talk.

With a little splutter, I managed, "What—what are you doing in my apartment?"

"Really? That's your question?" Sarah's voice pitched high. "I just told you there's a stranger in your house!"

"He's...not a stranger," I finished in a barely audible whisper. Clearing my throat, I tried for redirection again. "Why are you there?"

"Because you're my best friend and I care about you! You've basically gone off-grid since you got back from Europe, and I wanted to pop by and make sure you were okay!"

"I am. I'm fine. I'm great."

"You are in so much trouble right now," she warned. "Seriously, how could you not tell me you had a boyfriend?"

"I...well, I just..."

"Get your butt home right now!"

"Why don't we catch up this weekend and I can..."

"I am not leaving this guy alone in your apartment."

Drooping my head with a sigh, I muttered, "Okay, fine. I'm coming. Just be nice until I get there. He's a really great guy."

Sarah responded by hanging up on me, a true sign of just how pissed she was.

Wincing with a hiss, I packed up my stuff, urging myself to hurry. Poor Harry was probably getting the cold stare from my bestie, and although she's usually a happy ray of sunshine, she's pretty good at the icy stare-down.

As I scrambled to pack away my things, I imagined the scenario. Harry squirming in his bare feet while Sarah clipped around him in some gorgeous pair of heels she'd probably found at some rare shoe shop while researching for her next wedding client.

Rushing to my car, I drove the fastest way home, only getting caught briefly in the tail end of rush-hour traffic. Thirty minutes later, I was walking in my apartment door, shocked to find Justin there as well.

Blake's brother.

I wondered what he thought about all this.

From the grim look on his face, not much. In fact, he looked a mix of highly unimpressed and maybe a little wounded.

They all turned to look at me. Harry's eyes rounded with a *get me the hell out of this* kind of plea. I gave him a weak smile and cleared my throat as I placed my bag on the floor.

"So, I take it you've met?" I inched across to him while scratching my forearm and avoiding eye contact.

Sarah's icy blues were stripping me bare. "Yeah. We've met."

I forced a smile but it didn't quite rise. Sarah's glare switched to dismay, matching her husband perfectly. "How could you not tell me about this?"

"I'm sorry. I…" I pointed at Harry then back to her. "We met while I was in England and he came with me to France and…"

"You told me you were traveling alone!"

"I didn't think you'd be cool with the fact I was tripping around Europe with a guy I barely knew. You were dealing with your stuff." I pointed between her and Justin, ignoring Harry's confused expression. "And I was trying to deal with mine."

Sarah's lips spread into a stubborn line. "You should have told me."

I looked away from her, my jaw working to the side before I managed to whisper, "How?"

Her eyes glassed with tears, and she blinked then looked across to Justin. He walked over to her, gently rubbing her shoulders and kissing the side of her head.

Harry still looked confused, and I didn't have it in me to try to explain it all. I couldn't go into Blake's death and Justin and Sarah's almost divorce. I didn't want to relive it again.

An awkward, horrible silence descended on the room, and I wasn't sure how to fix it.

I kind of wanted them to leave. I felt awful for thinking that, because Sarah was my best friend, but Harry hadn't touched my past. He didn't know about Blake. The only stories he knew were ones from my childhood—safe ones that caused laughter, not tears.

I didn't want my past tainting what we had, but did that mean excluding people I cared about?

Sensing Harry's gaze on me, I turned to him with a hopeless smile. He gave me a sad, closed-mouth grin. Then with his usual charm, he killed the silence.

His hands made a loud snap as they clapped together. Everyone flinched and stared at him.

"I don't know about you guys, but this oppressive silence is getting kind of heavy. So, as awkward as it will no doubt be, why don't you lovely people stay for dinner? I'll even let you interrogate me so you can work out whether I'm good enough for your sweet Jane. Not sure which one of you is going to play bad cop, but I promise I'll be as honest as I can be. No nastiness required." He winked at Sarah, who was contemplating a bemused smile—I could tell by the wrinkling of her forehead.

Justin was still pretty reticent, but he finally gave in with a short nod and mumbled, "I'll order Indian."

"Fab. I love a good chicken tikka masala." Harry grinned.

Justin gave him an odd look before pulling out his phone and turning away to order.

Sarah, although cautious, seemed to relax a little and shuffled over to the table. Pulling out one of the three chairs, she sat and gave me a pointed look.

I bit back my smile, finding her motherly glares somewhat amusing now that the tense fog had lifted. Taking a seat beside her, it occurred to me that we'd be one chair short. It made my throat restrict. Since moving in, I'd only ever had two visitors at a time—my parents or Justin and Sarah. Much to my depression, I'd never needed a fourth chair.

But right then, I did.

I couldn't decide how I felt about that.

Harry closed his laptop and slipped it into his bag by the bed. Sarah watched him, her eyes darting to the bed before back to me.

Oh man, I had so much to tell her.

We used to talk about everything until Blake died and it all changed. I turned into a robot, she turned into a workaholic, and then all that shit went down between her and Justin, nearly killing their marriage. The last year had been nothing but a suck-fest. That was why I'd wanted the new year to be fresh and untainted.

I didn't want the old to mar it, but I couldn't just turn my back on Sarah, which meant the old would somehow have to find a place in my new life.

My heart hitched, my breathing growing rapid as Blake came to the forefront of my mind. I told him he'd be with me forever. But where'd he been the last week while I was making love to Harry and pretending like my soul mate didn't matter anymore?

Confusion made me frown and I scratched at the tabletop, unsure what to say.

Justin slid the phone back into his pocket and walked to the table. Nudging Sarah's arm, he quietly encouraged her to stand before slipping into her chair then nestling her on his knee. They shared a sweet look that I hadn't seen in a long time. It had more depth now. Nearly losing each other had brought them to a stronger place, and I could see the bond between them.

"So, would anyone like a drink?" Harry hovered behind me, still sounding a little nervous. "Tea? Beer? Wine?"

"Wine," Sarah and I said in unison.

We couldn't help sharing a brief smile before I glanced over my shoulder and spoke to Harry. "I think there's a red in the cupboard by the fridge."

"Got it." He puttered around behind me while I cautiously looked back at my friends.

We still weren't talking and it felt weird. Chatting with Sarah was usually as easy as breathing, but that was before I'd gone behind her back and fallen in love with a guy she didn't even know about.

Fallen in love.

Had I?

Was I?

Harry returned to the table, placing down a teacup and three wine glasses. He poured a generous amount into each glass then filled his teacup.

Lifting it, he proposed a quick toast. "To awkward conversations that will hopefully not end in my death or banishment."

I snorted and started to laugh as I raised my glass and decided...

Yes, I had fallen in love.

Harry made it impossible not to.

TWENTY

HARRY

In spite of the awkward start, I called our dinner with Justin and Sarah a success. Jane and I told them all about our trip. It was easy to go into detail, so many happy memories to recall. I then learned all about their wedding business, and I was even able to give Justin some tips on his website design.

It was nearly eleven o'clock.

Justin and I were sitting in front of my laptop looking at his website while Jane and Sarah giggled over dishes in the kitchen. "Counting Stars" was playing from Jane's portable speaker, and the girls started singing it together.

I glanced over at them. Jane and I had sung a lot in Nan's little Bambino, and the sound of her voice always made my insides warm.

I felt Justin's tension beside me and glanced back at him.

He'd been guarded the whole night, and I couldn't figure out why. I wasn't dumb enough to miss the fact that certain things hadn't been said. Throughout the meal, the three had shared frequent looks filled with meaning I didn't understand. Justin seemed to not mind me but something held him back, and rather than trying to guess, I decided to be bold and outright ask him.

"I get the distinct impression that you don't want to like me. Not that I'm here to impress you, but is there something I'm missing? Do I smell bad? Or is it my accent that puts you off?"

After a beat that felt way too long, he let out a breathy snicker and shook his head. "I-I'm sorry. It's j-just gonna take me s-some time to adjust to you."

"Right. And that's because…"

Justin's forehead wrinkled with confusion. "You don't know?"

"I'm pretty sure I wouldn't be looking at you like this if I did."

"H-how can you…" He shook his head. "It was s-such a big part of her life and she n-never said anything?"

I cleared my throat, his foreboding tone making my stomach coil. "Jane needed our trip to be nothing but fun, so we said no histories. I never expected to fall in love with her, and when I came over here, I didn't know how things would unfold. I guess I was kind of hoping history wasn't necessary to move forward."

Justin scoffed, anger taking the edge off his stutter. "Right, so we just pretend like he never existed? Nice."

His sharp, snappy tone made me flinch.

Never existed?

The inkling I'd been fighting surged forward. I glanced over my shoulder to stare at the guitar.

"Who was he?" I whispered.

Letting out a slow sigh, Justin waited until I was facing him before telling me everything I didn't want to know. "He was my brother, B-Blake. He got together with Jane in college and they were p-perfect. Everything was perfect," he murmured, and then his lips dipped into a sad frown. "Until he d-died...just before their wedding."

I closed my eyes, feeling sick as Justin muttered something about an accident. He didn't go into detail, and I didn't want to ask. My ears were ringing, turning his explanation to fuzz.

Staring across the room at Jane, I felt her pain like it was my own.

She'd lost the love of her life...just like I had.

I couldn't talk much after that. As soon as the dishes were done, Sarah was ready to leave, and it was an effort forming a smile as I said goodbye to the couple.

Pulling the tea towel off her shoulder, Jane hung it over the oven door and gave me a relieved smile.

"That went better than I expected. Thank God! You were amazing and brilliant and…" Her voice petered off as she caught sight of my face. "What's wrong?"

I couldn't hide it from her.

I didn't even want to.

"Justin told me about Blake."

Jane blanched then spun to scowl at the door. "He had no right to do that."

"I needed to know."

"No!" She spun back to face me, anguish bunching her cheeks and making her eyes glassy. "We said no histories!"

"Yeah, when it was a two-week holiday and I never thought I'd fall in love with you." I stepped toward her, my voice soft with sympathy. "Jane, that must have nearly killed you."

"Yes. It did," she clipped. "And I can't think about it. I can't bring him into this room with us." Tears slid down her cheeks as she tapped her chest. "He'll always own a piece of my soul, and I don't know how to let you both in. I don't know how to do this." Her voice pitched high, fear whisking away her last few words.

Gently touching her shoulder, I ran my hand down to her elbow then guided her to my chest. She sucked in a ragged breath, resting her cheek against me. Her tears dribbled onto my shirt as I held the side of her head and brushed my lips across her forehead.

"I get it, Jane. I understand."

"Do you?" She ripped out of my embrace,

shoving me away from her. "Really? Do you know what it's like to have your heart ripped out of your chest? To lose someone you thought you'd be with for the rest of your life?"

"Yes." I could barely choke out the word.

She froze, her green eyes vibrant as she waited for an explanation I never wanted to give her.

Would she still want me to stay if she knew the truth?

Swallowing down the thick lump in my throat, I began in a husky voice that gave away how close to the surface my pain still was. "I lost my girlfriend. We had a fight. I wouldn't do what she wanted me to. I told her maybe we needed a little space to figure it out, assuming that we'd both go blow off some steam then say sorry and talk…and kiss…and keep going." My eyes began to burn, and I squeezed them shut. "She slammed out of the apartment and tore away in her car…and never made it back." My voice began to tremble. "I switched off my phone because I didn't want to argue anymore. I… It was hours, and then when I turned it back on it rang straightaway. The police had been trying to get in touch to tell me…" My voice cut off as I fought tears that threatened to demolish me. I managed to pull it together, sniffing loudly before snapping out a quick finish. "She died on impact, apparently."

That was all I could say.

Our last words to each other had been in anger.

My sweet Tammy never made it back home because I was a stubborn asshole who refused to marry her.

TWENTY-ONE

JANE

I couldn't breathe.

I just stood there gaping at him while he shakily told me the truth. Tears continued to stream down my face, but they weren't for me. I was crying for the desolate look on Harry's face, the regret in his tear-drenched eyes.

"I'm sorry," I eventually managed to whisper.

"I can't remember the last thing I said to her, but she walked out of our place in tears, and I will regret that for the rest of my life." He closed the space between us, gripping my shoulders and beseeching me with a look I couldn't turn away from. "I had to come find you because I can't live with regret anymore. I have to cherish every moment I can. And even though it sometimes terrifies me, I need to be here with you, Jane. I need to love you. I know you don't know how to do this. I know you're scared, but please…let me stay."

A breathy sob punched out of me as I grabbed his face and leaned my forehead against his nose. Closing my eyes, I focused on the feel of his hands gently gliding down to my waist, his warm breath on my skin, the sound of his sniff as he fought his own anguish.

"I want you to stay," I finally whispered. "I need you to stay."

His lips hit mine the second the words were out of my mouth. Lifting me off the floor, he held me against him while I wrapped my legs around his waist. Our kisses were loud with fervor as he walked us to the bed.

I knew we were about to make love, but this time somehow felt different. It wasn't fun and flirty, fueled by lust. When I pulled the shirt over his head and ran my fingers down his body, I wasn't thinking about the pleasure it would bring me. I just wanted to be connected to him. I wanted him inside me so we could be one. I wanted to feel his pain, to fuse us together in a way we never had been before.

Straddling his legs, I played with his curls while he unbuttoned my dress all the way until it opened like a shirt. Slipping it off my shoulders, he then unhooked my bra. It dropped off the edge of the bed, and I watched it fall as his lips came around my nipple.

I felt like I was falling too.

Diving into something deeper than I had before.

I should have been whispering "Geronimo" with a smile, but I couldn't do anything more than close my eyes and kiss the top of his head as he sucked and licked my sensitive skin.

His lips traveled to my shoulder and I kissed his neck, my tears drying as I focused on pleasuring him.

We worked slowly, our movements languid like we were swimming in a deep pool. When he entered me, I didn't let out a loud cry; I just squeezed his shoulder and continued staring into his eyes as I rode him.

He sat against the pillows, holding my hips and showing me things he never had before. His eyes told me how much he'd suffered, and I let him in on a little of my own. As the tears built on my lashes, I leaned forward to kiss him, wanting our lovemaking to wash it all away.

Our mouths trembled against each other and he held my face, steadying me as we built to climax. My hips began to move at a faster pace, my body taking over as an orgasm tore through me. I moaned into his mouth, and he pulled me down on top of him. I could feel him trying to leave a part of himself behind, and I suddenly wished he wasn't wearing a condom.

The thought made me still.

Did I wish it?

As my heart simmered down to its usual rhythm, I sat back and gazed into Harry's face. His smile was gentle, his eyes filled with a depth of love I hadn't seen from him before.

In spite of this, fear still niggled, trying to break the spell we were under. After losing Blake I never thought I'd give so much of myself away…and so easily too.

But Harry made everything easy.

"Do you think we're going to make it?" I whispered.

Harry opened his mouth to respond, but the music did it for him. I hadn't even been aware it was still playing, but as his lips rose into a smile and he turned to look at the speaker in the kitchen, I stopped to listen to the song.

"Odds Are" by Barenaked Ladies.

It had been Blake's favorite band when we were in college, and they'd grown on me over the years we were together.

The chorus kicked in, and we both stilled to listen. Harry's eyes continued to glisten with affection as he ran his fingers down my face and smiled at me.

I let out a breathy laugh, the song being everything I needed to hear…and giving me the courage to whisper words I never thought I'd say to another man again.

"I love you."

TWENTY-TWO

HARRY

Someone's phone was ringing.

The buzz and ring breached my dreamlike daze, pulling me out of sleep. I groaned and rolled over, patting the nightstand and nearly dropping my phone on the floor. I slapped the hardware against the wood to stop it from falling and realized that it wasn't my phone that was ringing.

I placed my phone back on the nightstand and rolled the other way.

Jane groaned softly, coming out of sleep herself as I reached over her and grabbed the offending phone. I wanted to switch the bloody thing off and throw it across the room, but I doubted Jane would appreciate it.

My eyes were too blurry to read the screen, but I swiped to answer anyway.

"I have no bloody idea what time of the morning it is, but I can tell you—whoever you are—that it's too bloody early!"

The thought that it might be her mother suddenly occurred to me and I winced. I'd only met the woman a couple of times, and I couldn't afford to tarnish the good impression I'd been making.

"I know, I'm sorry. Is Jane there?" The man's voice was deep, American.

Jerking up, I snapped into the phone. "Who is this?"

Jane flicked on the light and squinted at me before grabbing her watch and looking at the time. "Are you kidding me? Who is that?"

"It's Troy," the man spoke into my ear. Jane had mentioned the name before—a work colleague. My insides settled to a simmer, but I still felt on edge. Why was a work colleague calling her in the early hours of the morning? "You must be Harry. I'm really sorry to call you this late, but it's urgent. It's about one of Jane's students."

His tone was ominous, making my gut clench. I'd experienced an ominous phone call before and it nearly killed me. I glanced at Jane then lowered my voice. "Is everything all right?"

"Look, I'm not sure. I hope it's gonna be."

"I'm not passing the phone over until I know

what's going on. I'm sure you can understand why."

Troy sighed. "One of her students is missing. She took off sometime in the night, and her parents are freaking out. I'm just calling to see if Jane can help."

"Is it Brandy?" I flicked the covers off my legs and jumped out of bed.

"What are you doing?" Jane's voice rose with panic. I glanced at her wide green eyes and realized how alarming my sudden movements probably were. "Who are you talking to?"

Switching the phone onto speaker, I dropped it on the bed and started getting dressed.

"Her dad went to check on her before he went to bed at eleven, and her room was empty."

Jane gasped. "Brandy?"

"Yeah, hi, Jane." Troy's voice sounded heavy and tired. "Can you give me any ideas?"

She scrambled out of bed and pulled a pair of sweatpants over her pajamas.

"I'm not sure. She seemed fine when I spoke to her at the end of the day."

"Yeah, well, her world got thrown sideways when she got home from school."

"Why?" Jane's head popped out from her sweater while I started lacing my shoes.

"Her mom won the case. Looks like she'll be moving to Chile soon."

"Oh no," Jane whispered. "Where have you looked so far?"

"The police and a team of volunteers are

scouring the neighborhood. It's been hours and we're getting kind of desperate. I've searched the twenty-four eateries within a five-mile radius."

"Have you tried the school?" Jane grabbed the phone off the bed and ran for her keys.

"It's locked up tight. How would she even get in?"

"I don't know, but that's where I'm starting."

"Okay. I'll finish my drive through this part of town then head over there to join you."

"Call me if anything changes."

"Will do."

Jane slipped the phone into her pocket then, with her hand on the door, spun back to look at me. "You don't have to come if you don't want."

"Jane," I softly chided. "Of course I'm coming with you."

As she led the way to the car, I couldn't help being surprised at the fact she'd even questioned my company. It was a crisis. As if I'd let her go off and deal with it alone.

My gut twisted as I thought ahead to the following week. I was due to fly back to England, and I didn't have a definite date of return. I was planning to make it as soon as bloody possible after Nan's birthday celebrations, but it wouldn't be soon enough.

I didn't want to leave Jane.

The thought of her living in her little apartment without me, dealing with three a.m. phone calls on her own...it near killed me.

I wanted to be with Jane not just for a

holiday…or an elongated stay…but for life.

In the past that thought would have terrified me. Nothing was certain. My parents were supposed to be married for life, and Dad abandoned us all for five years. It was complete shit and the very reason I shied away from making any kind of commitment that could potentially hurt someone. I wasn't about false claims.

That's why I'd refused Tammy.

But I didn't want to make the same mistakes again.

I wanted to be there for Jane, from the mundane grocery shopping to the convertible cruises to Malibu…to the ulcer-inducing stress of searching for a confused twelve-year-old kid who was no doubt scared out of her wits.

TWENTY-THREE

JANE

We didn't speak as we tore through the street. Traffic was light, making the trip to school a fast one. My insides were going nuts.

One of my students was missing.

Missing!

Thoughts of what kind of trouble she could have gotten into nearly blinded me as I ran a red then careened around the corner.

"It's going to be okay." Harry's voice was so soft and calm.

"How do you know that!" I snapped. "You don't!"

"You're right." He nodded, still frustratingly calm. "I don't. I'm just trying to have a little faith."'

I scoffed, shaking my head as I gripped the wheel.

"I know you're scared," he whispered. "I get it. We both know firsthand that life isn't perfect, but I'm not going to torture myself by worrying about something that may not have happened yet."

Sucking in a shaky breath, I started blinking at my tears.

"Brandy's a smart kid. We have to trust that."

"I just…" My voice wobbled. "I can't do it again, you know?"

He knew what I was saying. I didn't have the strength to survive another tragedy.

My trembling words shut him up, and he gripped my leg a little tighter.

My mind immediately jumped to Blake and the way I felt as I sat in my wedding dress, trying to wrap my head around the fact my groom was no longer on his way.

Stealing a quick glance at Harry's pale face, I had to assume he was thinking about the girlfriend he'd lost. Neither of us had gone into details about our respective partners. I didn't want to know about her, and he didn't seem overly interested in learning about Blake.

We shared yet another thing in common— broken hearts. It made the desire to simply be happy together and enjoy each other that much stronger.

We'd spent a few moments whispering into the

darkness, reliving how it felt when we first heard the news—his dreaded phone call, me listening to my mother's quivering voice—but neither of us had delved further.

Jerking to a stop in the street, I switched off the engine and lurched out of the car. Harry took my hand and we ran to the school gate together.

Wrapping his hands around the metal, he looked up and muttered, "Climbable. Very climbable."

My fingers were trembling as I unlocked the padlock with my key and pulled the gate open.

"Brandy!" Harry started calling the second we reached the main entrance.

Leading him around to the side door, I let us in and joined his call.

"Brandy! Are you in here?"

Our voices blended together as we raced down the hallways, checking each door. Most of them were locked, except for the bathrooms.

I took the girls' while Harry checked the boys'. My sneakers squeaked on the white tiles as I checked each stall.

"Jane! Get in here!" Harry's muffled shout made me flinch.

I nearly slipped as I raced out the door. Harry was waiting for me with the boys' bathroom door wide open. I followed him down to the last stall and noticed the smashed glass all over the toilet. A few smears of blood painted the tank.

"Shit," I murmured.

"She must have cut herself getting in." Harry

squeezed my shoulder. Maybe he could see the pulse throbbing in my neck. My heart was acting crazy, hammering with fear as I stared at the blood. "But it means she's probably here."

It took me a second to register his words. I glanced up at his hopeful smile, my head bobbing erratically. "Let's go."

"Brandy!" we yelled together, taking a side of the hall each and trying every single doorknob. I called Troy, and he assured me he'd make all the right phone calls while Harry and I continued to look.

"Every bloody door's locked!" Harry's face bunched with desperation.

"The janitor's coming with his set of keys."

"I know. I'd just like to find her before she's swamped by a truckload of people fussing over her. Most people naturally go into hiding when they're dealing with bad news. I'm guessing she's no different."

I remembered the way I'd shrunk in on myself when Blake first died. So many people had tried to be there for me, and I'd shut them out in my systematic, robotic way.

"Let's keep looking." I took his hand, leading him down the next hallway.

We reached my classroom and I tried the handle, but the door was locked. I was about to run away from it but jerked to a stop.

"You okay?" Harry turned back when my hand slipped out of his.

"I have a key. I can at least check this room."

Fumbling my key chain, I struggled to shove the correct key into the lock.

"Just take a breath, love."

I closed my eyes and did as Harry told me, sliding the key into the lock and pushing my door open. It creaked, sounding ominous in the dark hours of the morning.

Flicking on my light, I squinted against the sudden brightness and stepped into the room.

"Brandy? Are you in here?" My voice was flat.

I guess I expected nothing in response.

But then I heard a faint sniff.

Harry and I both flinched still, our heads snapping toward my desk. It was only then that I noticed my chair was pushed out further than it usually would be.

"Brandy? It's Harry." He slowly approached the front of the classroom.

Her only response was a slight rustling of clothing and another sniff.

Pulling the chair away, Harry crouched down, the gentle smile on his face enough to make me certain I was in love with him.

"Hey, runaway," he whispered.

Brandy let out a little whimper, and her sniffs turned into pitiful cries. I rushed around the side of the desk, kneeling down as Harry gently pulled her out of hiding.

She wrapped her skinny arms around his neck and hung on tight while he rubbed her back and shushed her.

I placed my hand next to his, stroking her

shoulder as she cried against him.

There were scratches on her forearms, nothing too deep. She'd need patching up, but nothing a Band-Aid and cuddle couldn't cure. Relief swirled through me, and I slumped to the floor.

Brandy pulled out of Harry's embrace to look at me. Her sad brown eyes were so large and uncertain.

"You scared me." I tried to smile at her. "I thought we'd lost you for good. Why'd you run?"

Troy had told me, but I wanted to hear her version.

"I'm moving to Chile." Her voice wobbled, and she sucked in a ragged breath. "Dad's so upset," she hiccupped. "He was yelling at Mom and crying. I've never seen him cry before. I don't know what to do. I have to go with her, but how do I leave him?"

Harry gave me a pained frown, his eyes glassing over as he blinked and rocked her on his knee.

"I know it sucks," he finally managed. "I wish I could say something amazing to make this all better."

She sniffed and cried some more while I texted Troy to let him know we'd found her.

We heard him running down the hall a few minutes later. His entire body sagged with relief when he spotted us on the floor by my desk.

"Thank you, God," he breathed, then walked across to us.

Brandy sucked in a breath and looked up at him, a fresh wave of tears filling her eyes.

"I'm sorry, B," Troy murmured.

She nodded, her blotchy face crumpling as she rested her head against Harry's shoulder again. "I know running was dumb, but I just couldn't listen to him crying anymore. Why should she get me when he's not allowed to? I just figured it'd be more fair if they both went without me."

"I know." Troy's voice, although deep, was always so soft and reassuring. "You shouldn't even have to be in this position. Life's not fair."

"I don't want to go! And I don't want to stay! I just... I want to be a family again!"

"That's not going to happen. You know that." The look on Troy's face told me they'd had this chat before. "But you've got two parents who are going out of their minds with worry right now, which tells me that you've got two parents who really love you. And even though they can't be together anymore, it doesn't change how they feel about you."

"Sounds like they need you," I added.

Brandy's gaze hit mine, and I gave her an understanding smile. Her response was a slightly surly lip curl.

"Before you say, *what do you know about it*, I can assure you that I *do* know about it. I know what it feels like to say goodbye to someone you're not ready to leave. But you have some pretty awesome things going for you. Skype, FaceTime, WhatsApp. There are so many cool ways to keep in touch with your dad, and I'm sure he's already working out when he can come down and visit."

"It's not the same," she grumbled.

"I know," I croaked, catching Harry's eye and getting a taste of what he was thinking.

That'd be us soon. It was better than nothing, but it wouldn't be the same as having him in my bed each night.

Dammit. I was gonna miss him so bad.

That thought paired with Brandy's anguish made tears pop onto my lashes. I tried to blink them away, but it didn't work. Tears trickled down my face as I gave Harry a sorrowful smile. His expression mirrored mine, but we kept it all in.

That moment wasn't about our impending separation. It was about Brandy.

Sniffing at my egotistical tears, I swiped them off my face and stood. "Come on, your parents will be waiting."

Scooping her up, Harry stood and cradled her in his arms. She held tight to his neck as we walked to the front of the school. The second we reached the doors, her mother appeared, slamming out of her car and running across to rip Brandy from Harry's grasp.

"My baby. You had me worried sick," she sobbed and clung to her daughter. Brandy's father appeared out of the darkness, his face smeared with tears as he gripped his mouth and watched his daughter and ex-wife embrace. His expression was a blend of relief and dismay. He'd found his baby girl but had to prepare himself to say goodbye for real.

Gliding his arm across my shoulders, Harry

pulled me against him and kissed the top of my head. I snuggled into him, cherishing his touch. In a few short days I wouldn't have it anymore.

And I didn't know how I was going to live without it.

Just like Brandy's father, I wasn't sure how I was going to prepare myself to say goodbye for real.

TWENTY-FOUR

HARRY

I couldn't believe how quickly six weeks had passed. When I'd first touched down in LA, I wasn't sure how long I'd be there.

But Jane had invited me in, and it'd been the best time I'd had.

Living with her was easy.

Being part of her life felt incredibly natural, and I couldn't believe I was just walking away from that.

Nan was important to me though. I had a life in England, and I couldn't pretend it didn't exist.

Jane held my hand as we walked to the security

checkpoint. Her jaw trembled slightly when she clenched it, and I swear my heart was about to start bleeding.

"You sure you don't want to come with me?" I tried again.

She snickered then sniffed. "You know I can't. My next break isn't until Thanksgiving...and you'll be back before then, right?"

"Of course. I'll save as hard and as fast as I can. I've already taken on a couple of extra clients. It won't be long." I tried to give her an encouraging smile, but that wouldn't change the fact that even if I did come back, I'd be on limited time.

Goodbyes were inevitable in our future together.

Unless...

My throat thickened with emotion, making it hard to swallow...nearly impossible to get the words out. I gazed down at her beautiful face, smiling at the sprinkling of freckles on her pale skin, loving the curve of her cheek and the intensity of her emerald stare.

Yes, I could do it.

I could say it...and I could mean it.

My voice came out in a husky whisper as I said the words I'd always feared. "Marry me."

Her eyes rounded as I pulled her against me and threaded my fingers behind her back. "What?"

"I don't want to have to keep leaving you. This time's hard enough. It'll be even worse next time because I'll have to stay away for longer." I shone her a hopeful smile. "And Georjana Tindal has a wonderful ring to it, don't you think?"

Her laughter was made breathy with surprise. "Harry, I..." She shook her head and bit her lip.

"You know you want to."

I probably sounded like such a desperate idiot, but I knew she loved me.

The sad smile on her face made my heart twist out of shape.

"Harry," she whispered, dipping her head and breaking eye contact. Resting her forehead against my shoulder she tried to break my heart. "I can't get married again. I can't do that whole wedding planning thing and the anticipation and then the..." She stopped breathing, holding on to the things she was too afraid to say.

I nudged her cheek with my nose. "We don't have to plan a wedding. Let's just elope to some island and do it. Or better yet, go to a courthouse."

"How romantic." Her droll expression made me grin.

"We don't need a big wedding. You and me together, that *is* romance. We're meant to be."

My words were weakening her, I could tell by her wobbly smile and the way she struggled to refute me. Her mouth opened and closed a couple of times, but she shook her head again. "Are you just doing this to get a green card?"

I laughed and kissed her lips. Leaning back, I brushed her hair behind her ear and made sure she was looking into my eyes. "I'm doing this because I love you. Say yes, Jane."

Her erratic breath hit my chin and she bruised

my heart with a pained smile. "I...don't know."

Refusing to let her hesitation bring me down, I held the back of her head and kissed her with everything I had. I poured my heart into the moment, desperate for her to know how much I meant it.

Out of breath, I pulled back and gazed down at her. "Did that help persuade you at all?"

Her red lips smiled, and her eyes glassed with tears as she chuckled. "Nearly."

I couldn't leave her crying, so I kept the moment as light as I could. "Okay, fine. You don't have to say yes." Reluctantly letting her go, I stood back and pointed at her. "But if you miss me, if you yearn for me in your bed, then I'm expecting a yes next time I see you."

She laughed. "Well, I might as well just say yes right now, because I know I'm going to miss you." Grabbing my collar, she yanked me back for a kiss.

Our tongues danced together, a last passionate tango to see us through until the next time.

Pressing her forehead against mine, she whispered against my lips, "And I know I'm going to yearn for you in my bed."

Her words made me warm all the way to my toes. Touching her cheek, I gazed into those stunning green eyes and went for the honest truth. "I don't want to force you into a yes, and I know I'll be sharing your heart, just like you're sharing mine...but I've got space for you, darling. And I don't want to regret not asking."

The leaving her not crying thing was going to be

impossible. Tears welled so high in her eyes they spilled over her lashes, but the affectionate joy in her gaze gave me the courage to leave her.

Stopping at the checkpoint, I spun one last time and blew her a kiss.

"I love you," I mouthed, and placed my hand on my heart.

She mirrored me and mouthed, "I love you too."

Staring at her for a second longer, I memorized everything I could before turning away and taking her with me in my heart.

TWENTY-FIVE

JANE

Breathing on the way back to my apartment was a struggle. I couldn't move past Harry's proposal.

Marriage.

It felt so big…and yet the idea of being with him was so incredibly natural.

I should have said yes on the spot, but…

Fear twisted through me, eating at my insides until I pulled my car into its parking spot and was swamped with a depressing wave of loneliness.

For the last six weeks, every time I walked up the steps and into my apartment Harry was either beside me or there when I opened the door.

The apartment would be so quiet without him. I wasn't sure I'd ever get used to living alone. I'd moved out because living with my parents got to be too much after the funeral, but I never liked it.

"So why can't you say yes, you big idiot!" Resting my forehead on the steering wheel, I let out a frustrated scream.

I needed logic to kick in and tell me every reason I shouldn't marry a man I'd known for less than three months. It would be completely crazy. I hadn't met any of his family yet. He'd met my parents a few times, but in spite of my mother's subtle probing, I was still too afraid to admit how much I loved him. Sarah and Justin had been the only ones we let in, and although Justin remained slightly aloof, we'd had some great meals together.

Harry was pretty charming and hard to resist.

But...

Slamming out of my car, I stormed up the stairs and into my apartment. The door shook as I smacked it closed behind me. I kind of wanted that to feel better, but it didn't. Spinning around, I faced my empty apartment and screamed.

Because it wasn't empty.

Sarah's smile was tender with understanding as she pushed the dining chair out beside her and pointed at it. "Sit down. Let's drink tea."

"I'd rather drink vodka shots," I grumbled, dumping my bag on the corner of the table and slumping into my seat.

Sarah got up to retrieve the kettle and poured boiling water over my waiting teabag.

Placing the mug in front of me, she gave my shoulder a little rub. "You knew it was going to be a tough day. Saying goodbye always sucks, especially when you don't have a return date to look forward to."

I dunked my teabag up and down, focusing on the rhythmic motion while I worked up the courage to confess, "He asked me to marry him."

"What!" Sarah's blue eyes bulged as she banged her teacup back on the table. Liquid jumped out, splashing my legs and making me yelp. "Sorry! Sorry." She rushed over to the sink, grabbing a cloth and quickly returning to clean up.

Patting my leg dry, she then wiped the table while verbally gushing. "Oh my gosh, that's so amazing."

"You're happier about it than I am!"

Sarah looked at me with a bemused frown. "Why aren't you happy?"

"Because it's totally insane! He's been in my life for like a second."

"So?"

I gave her a pointed look. "Sarah, come on. You don't rush into these things. I can't just impulsively marry this man."

"But you guys are so great together. You make it look so easy and natural, like you've known each other for years. Isn't that what marriage is supposed to be like?"

"It's not..." I shook my head, scrambling to argue with her. Her points were really good. Being with Harry was as easy as breathing.

Sarah's eyes sparkled while she studied me. "I like him, Janey."

"You like everybody," I muttered.

She chuckled and placed her hand on my arm. "No, I really like *him*. And more importantly, I like you when you're around him."

I went still, slowly looking up to meet her gaze.

"He brings out the best in you."

"You used to say that about Blake."

Sarah shrugged and picked up her tea. "He did too. That doesn't mean Harry can't as well."

My shoulders drooped and I slumped back into my chair. "I always thought Blake was my soul mate. How is it possible to fall in love with someone else? What would he think of all this?"

"Sweetie." Sarah placed her mug down and leaned across the table, squeezing my hand. "I wish it didn't have to be this way, but Blake's not here. He may live on in our hearts, but he will never physically be here again."

I closed my eyes, absorbing her words. They felt harsh in spite of the fact they were said with such compassion.

"Harry is here…and he wants you. He makes you happy. And I know you'll always love Blake, but he doesn't get to have an opinion on this one. You need to live for *you* now. Wasn't that the whole point of going overseas, to figure out how to get by without him? Well, life figured it out for you."

"I just…don't know." My last two words came out in a squeak, fear cutting off my air supply.

"Okay." Sarah sat back, her eyes narrowing as she studied my face. "What's making you hesitate?"

I shook my head, words failing me as I tried to answer the question. I opened my mouth then clenched my jaw. Squeezing my eyes shut, I took a breath before blurting, "What if something goes wrong? What if he starts to hate me or he starts to drive me insane! What if something comes between us?" I opened my eyes and let her see the root of my doubts. "What if he dies?"

Sarah's eyes started to mist, matching my anguished look.

"When Blake and I were together, it didn't even occur to me that something bad would happen. I was so full of hope, but now I know… I know what loss feels like, and I can't go through it again."

Swiping the tear off her face, Sarah sniffed and sat up straight. "I know it nearly killed you. It nearly killed Justin and me as well, but you have to listen to me. You cannot deprive yourself of joy for the rest of your life because you're scared you might lose it. What if you don't? What if you and Harry live to be one hundred and you die in a warm bed together?"

"The chances of that happening are so incredibly low."

"So are the chances of you losing him on your wedding day."

I looked away from Sarah's conviction, not sure I was brave enough to believe it.

"What happened to you is awful and thankfully

rare. Do you honestly think you'd have to live through it twice?"

"Good people have horrible things happen to them all the time."

"Yes." She nodded. "But they also have good things happen to them. Life will only beat you down if you let it. You had the love of your life ripped away from you, and you'd convinced yourself you'd never love again. And then Harry came along. He makes you so happy. You have laughed more with him than you've ever laughed with anybody...even Blake."

My eyes snapped up to connect with hers. Anger sparked through me as I tried to deny it, but I couldn't. Harry did make me laugh. He was funny and charming, and I loved being with him.

Wrapping my fingers around my mug, I took a quick sip. Logic had kicked in just the way I wanted it to, but it was telling me the most unexpected thing. It was filling my brain with all the reasons I should be saying yes. Shouting it from the rooftops even.

A smile tugged at the edge of Sarah's mouth while she watched me. I flicked my eyes to hers, and she jumped out of her chair. "Yes! Yes! This is so exciting!"

I looked at my watch, breaths punching out of me as I tried to calculate what time Harry's flight left and when I'd be able to call him.

"So, his flight is about ten hours, which means he'll land...when? What time will it be if I call?"

With a jerk, Sarah stopped happy dancing and

pointed at me. "Oh, you are so not saying yes over the phone."

"Well, how else am I supposed to do it?"

With a glinting smile, she leaned down, resting her hand on the table and getting right in my face. "In person, of course."

"I can't get out of work."

Sarah sighed, and pursed her lips. "Wait!" She snapped her fingers. "It's Columbus Day next week. If you could get out of school early on Friday, I could drive you to the airport to catch an afternoon flight. You'll arrive in London the next day, go to Rye, say yes, meet his family, make love all night, then he'll take you back to London and you'll be home in time for school on Tuesday."

"You are a crazy person." I gave her a pointed look.

Her tongue stuck out the side of her mouth, her smile all-knowing. "I thought crazy was your thing these days."

It was her wriggling eyebrows that did it.

They forced a smile over my lips, and then a squeal popped out of my mouth. Before I knew it, I was happy dancing behind her back while she called the airline and arranged it all for me.

Crazy.

Totally crazy.

And I'd never been so happy and terrified in my entire life.

TWENTY-SIX

HARRY

"Would you smile? You're making me want to slit my throat." Renee threw her coaster at me. It pinged off my nose and dropped to the table.

I gave my sister a dark scowl and rubbed the sore spot.

"Don't look at me like that. I finally get an afternoon off and I choose to spend that precious, kid-free time at the pub with my hilarious brother and you've yet to make one joke. Not even a funny quip when Travis Newhart walked past in leather pants." She leaned over the table, her eyebrows raised. "*Leather* pants on a sixty-year-old."

She stared at me expectantly, and I forced a half smile.

"Oh, you're pathetic."

"Sorry," I groaned. "I've just got a lot on my mind."

She let out a loud, cynical laugh, drawing a few eyes to our table. "A lot? No, you have one thing on your mind."

"Why won't she return my calls? It's been nearly two days."

"Harry, come on. Maybe something's happened to her phone—dead battery, dropped it down the loo, I don't know. But you can't get this depressed again. I won't have it." Her eyes flickered with concern as she reached across and squeezed my arm. "You nearly destroyed yourself last time. I can't see you go through it twice."

I gave her a glum smile. "I never wanted to fall in love again, but with Jane it's been the easiest thing I've ever done. I should never have asked her to marry me. I scared her off." I huffed, picking up Renee's coaster and fidgeting with the edge. "Ironic, isn't it? I lost Tammy because I wouldn't ask, and now I'm losing Jane because I did!"

"You're not losing her." Renee's voice softened to the tone she used with her kids. "She just hasn't returned your last call as quickly as you wanted her to."

"She was distant the last time I spoke to her. Something was wrong. She was acting edgy." I thumped the table. "This distance is going to kill me."

"Well, you're due to go back at the end of the month, aren't you?"

I scrubbed a hand down my face. "Yeah, as soon as I get paid for the Pullman job I'll have enough. Business was slower over the summer than I expected."

"And you spent basically all your money tripping around France, Spain, and Portugal like a wealthy man."

I gave her a dark look. "It was the trip of my life."

"Good. Then stop complaining about the fact you can't return to see your girl yet. Nan's face when you showed up for her party was worth coming home for. You have to admit that."

"Yeah, yeah, I do. I just wish…"

"I know. And I'm sorry you can't have everything, and I'm sorry no one in the family can afford to pay your airfare outright."

Leaning away from the table, Renee signaled for Devan to bring us another round.

"This one's on me." She winked and I loved her for it.

It was impossible to stay mad with my sister.

I was being a grumpy bastard, and yet she still sat with me. I guess I was just worried. Jane and I were so in love when we were together. Skype calls and texts weren't the same.

I already felt like she was slipping away from me, and it hadn't even been two weeks.

Picking up my phone, I checked the screen again. With a motherly tsk, Renee snatched it out of my hand and shoved it in her bag.

I went to reach for it but she pushed me away. "Just for an hour. Switch off, stop thinking, enjoy the band."

Knowing she was right, I closed my eyes and ran a hand through my hair. Different indie bands had been showcasing their talents throughout the afternoon. Most people were playing covers. One singer got up with an original song that wasn't bad. A band I didn't know was on the stage strumming out a tune that sounded like that band Jane liked, Barenaked Ladies.

"I'm gonna walk. I won't quit..."

The song of course made me think of Jane.

Had I really been contemplating giving up on her because of distance? I had to think of another way to reach her. I had to somehow convince her to marry me so we didn't have to keep leaving each other.

But what if she wouldn't?

What if she let fear win?

Renee cleared her throat. I ignored her, too absorbed by the questions thrumming through my brain.

"Harry." She nudged my elbow.

Again, I ignored her, keeping an eye on the band and letting the song inspire me.

"Useless brother," Renee sang. "I really think you should turn around and see who's just walked in."

"What?" I gave her a confused frown.

She tipped her head at the bar, and I turned in a

daze until I saw a shock of red hair and snapped up straight.

"Jane!" I called across the pub.

Turning at my startled cry, she found me easily, her face lighting like a beacon as she moved toward me. I stumbled off my stool, bumping into someone and having to quickly apologize before I could reach her.

She laughed and teased, "It's only four o'clock. Are you drunk already?"

"No," I whispered, grabbing her face and kissing her to make sure she was real.

She held my wrists and laughed into my mouth when a man wolf-whistled to my right.

Pulling away, I gazed down at her face, still cupping her cheeks. "What are you doing here?"

"I have to tell you something."

I held my breath, my heart drumming in my ears while her lips rose into the slowest, most triumphant smile I'd ever seen.

Removing my hands from her face, she rose to her tiptoes and whispered in my ear, "Yes."

"Yes?" I repeated, sounding like a total plonker.

"Yes."

I gasped and stepped back, holding her shoulders and looking into her eyes. "Yes." My head bobbed. "You just said yes."

"I did."

"And you meant it."

"Wouldn't have flown all this way if I hadn't."

"Of course you wouldn't have." I picked her up, squeezing her against me and spinning around until she laughed in my ear.

She placed her hands on my shoulders and grinned down at me. "This is so crazy."

"Which is so us."

"Yeah." She nodded and started laughing again.

I'd never seen her smile so bright, and I let out a whoop before I could stop myself. Placing her on the floor beside me, I shouted at the top of my voice, "I'm getting married!"

The entire pub paused for a shocked beat. Then Renee raised her beer in the air and yelled, "Go, Harry!"

Everyone joined her, raising their mugs and toasting us.

Jane's cheeks fired bright red, and she buried her face in the crook of my neck. I slung my arm across her shoulders and walked her over to my sister.

I had no idea how long she could stay, but it didn't even matter. Soon enough, we'd be connected for good, and oceans wouldn't be parting us.

If I could've had my way, I'd have married her that very night.

TWENTY-SEVEN

JANE

Harry and I spent the night celebrating. His older sister made a call, and within the hour every member of Harry's family had arrived at the pub—even his nan.

She was a fragile woman with keen eyes and a sharp wit. What she lacked in physicality, she made up for in intelligence. Her hands trembled as I chatted with her for most of the evening, figuring out why Harry loved her so much. It wasn't hard; she was adorable, and the bond between the two was obvious.

The rest of Harry's family was great too. I got to

meet all but Simon, who had already traveled back to Edinburgh after their family reunion the week before.

At around nine, we used Nan as an excuse to get home. Once she was safely upstairs, Harry took me down to his basement bedroom and made love to me. Not the rip-your-clothes-off kind when he'd turned up at my school, but the languid kind. He kissed every inch of my body, pleasuring me until I could barely breathe. When I woke in the early morning, I returned the favor, and the sun rose while I cried out on top of him with my legs wrapped around his waist.

He held me against him and spun us over. I loved the weight of him on top of me. His head flopped down on the pillow as he panted in my ear. "How am I supposed to take you to London today? I can't say goodbye to this."

I ran my hand up his back and kissed his shoulder. "It won't be for long. As soon as you fly into LA, we can go straight to the courthouse. Sarah and Justin can witness, and I'm sure Dad can help me work out any visa complications." Harry's eyes glistened as I bit my lips together then smiled. "We'll be legally bound. They'll have to let you stay."

"I like the sound of that." He covered my mouth with his lips, holding me close as we tried not to think about my impending departure that afternoon.

"So, are you sure you're happy to move to LA first, at least until I see the school year out?" I went into planning mode, the best way to cope.

"Of course. I can work from anywhere." He kissed my cheek and rolled off me. Resting his head on his knuckles, he gazed down at my face and started drawing circles around my breasts.

I lightly played with the fine hairs on his forearm. "What about your nan?"

"Renee and Mum can help look after her. She did fine while I was with you last time. If things get close to the edge, I'll just find the money to fly back. And with you as my wife—" He kissed my nose. "—you'll have the perfect excuse to come with me."

I smiled, loving the sound of it. Encouraged by how much it didn't terrify me.

Harry's wife. As long as I didn't think about the time between leaving him and marrying him, I could stay excited. At least it was short. I wouldn't be worrying about insignificant wedding details, the things that all became worthless the second Blake died.

It would be different.

Heck, I'd get married in jeans and a hoodie if I had to. I just wanted to be with Harry, and marrying him was the best way to do that. I loved him, so spending my life with him sounded like a pretty good plan to me.

Life.

Would we get that?

My stomach knotted as fear nibbled at the corners of my mind. It must have shown through in my gaze because Harry gave me a soft smile and whispered, "You're not going to lose me." He then started singing the chorus from "Odds Are," and I wondered if that would become our song.

I grinned at him with shimmering eyes until he'd finished the song, then kissed him until we were out of breath again.

Harry's alarm stopped us from taking things to the next level. Lifting his watch, he checked the time and murmured, "Got to go check on Nan, and I may as well get us breakfast while I'm up there, eh?"

"Tea would be wonderful. Thank you."

He kissed each of my breasts before he slid out of bed, then wiggled his cute butt to make me laugh. I didn't hide the fact I was checking him out as he pulled on a pair of sweats and headed up the stairs shirtless.

Flopping back onto my pillow, I let out a wistful sigh. He really was gorgeous—inside and out. A warm, giddy sensation twirled through me, that lightheaded buzz that comes with new love. I'd felt it with such intensity when I first started dating Blake. I never thought I'd feel it again.

It was different this time though.

Blake was like a god to me. At first, I felt like a giggling schoolgirl beside him until he'd finally convinced me that I wasn't playing out of my league.

But with Harry it was so easy. We were in each other's league, easy banter and conversation from the outset. None of that awkward flirting and worrying that he might not like me. We started as friends, and it just progressed into something more.

Maybe that's why falling for him was so easy…so natural.

Sitting up, I pushed the covers off me and padded across to the bathroom. After brushing my teeth and washing my face, I walked back into the room to get dressed. My little suitcase lay open against Harry's desk, and it made me sad to think I'd be zipping it up again in a few hours and heading to London.

Thanks to time zones and travel time, I only got one night.

All that way for one night.

A smile touched my lips as I recaptured the look on his face when he saw me standing in the pub…and the joy in his voice when he told everyone he was getting married.

It'd been worth it.

I'd spend the rest of the week exhausted, but it'd be worth it.

That excited, giddy buzz ate away at my fear, reminding me that everything would be okay. I didn't have to worry. My impulses were making me happy. I had to stop thinking so far ahead.

Life wasn't going to beat me up like last time.

Pulling on my sweats, I tied the waistband string then slid on a T-shirt before packing my meager belongings and settling on Harry's couch. Snatching my phone, I opened Spotify and pressed shuffle play on my "favorites" list. "Somebody To You" by The Vamps. I grinned. I loved that song.

I bobbed my head as I scanned the bedroom.

Harry's workspace was neat and organized, a good sign. I never did well with clutter, and if he was going to be working in my tiny studio apartment, he was going to have to be tidy. There was a shirt hanging out from his laundry hamper. I jumped up and put it in properly before spinning and dancing my way back to the couch.

With a satisfied sigh, I flopped back into the plump chair, propping my toes on the edge of the coffee table. A stack of design magazines sat in a crooked pile. I leaned forward and straightened it up, browsing the titles as I did so. They were all website design and artistic magazines. They looked interesting enough, but not as intriguing as the paperback novels on the shelf next to me.

They were old copies of the greats—*Pride and Prejudice, Great Expectations, Wuthering Heights*...the copy of *The Great Gatsby* that I read while in France and Spain. They must have been his nan's books.

With a smile, I ran my finger along them until I reached the end of the row.

Jane Austen was obviously a favorite. Pulling *Sense and Sensibility* free, I accidentally unearthed a waterfall of photos and letters that had been tucked at the end of the shelf.

"Whoops," I murmured, jumping out of the seat and crouching down to tidy them up.

I flipped over the top photo, which was framed in simple white wood, a sad ache ripping through me as I gazed at the young blonde. She had bright eyes and a cheery smile, small dimples in her round cheeks. She was sitting on a park bench, holding one of the old books I'd been admiring. I couldn't read the title, but I figured it was one from the shelf. I had to assume Harry took the picture and interrupted her reading with one of his charming jokes. Her smile was mid-laughter, open and beautiful.

Swallowing, I tucked the photo back in the shelf and continued gathering the other things. There were a few folded letters with "Harry" inside a love heart drawn on the outside. As tempted as I was, I didn't read them. Harry and I seemed to have an unspoken agreement that we didn't delve into each other's pasts, particularly where our lost loves were concerned. We just wanted to move on. Forward.

No looking back.

I stacked the papers in a neat pile then placed them back on the shelf, glad I hadn't been caught. I didn't want our last few hours to be tainted by an awkward conversation.

But then I spotted something I couldn't ignore.

A picture...a fuzzy black-and-white one that I'd seen before. It was surrounded by words, like a newspaper article.

With a frown, I reached for it, my heart spasming as I read the headline.

"Tragic Road Accident Makes Locals Question Tourist Driver Requirements."

The paper in my hand began to quiver as I tried to read the article, but I couldn't. Tears were blinding me, fueled by the black-and-white image of a mangled car askew on the side of the road.

The car that killed Blake.

TWENTY-EIGHT

HARRY

With a whistle, I carried the tray back downstairs. Nan was set up with her tea and toast. She'd actually been making it herself when I reached her, and she shooed me away from helping.

So I pottered beside her, keeping half an eye on her shaking hands while she slowly buttered her toast. She managed just fine.

Stealing the marmalade, I spread it over my piece then added strawberry jam to Jane's. I even spread it right to the edges, just the way she liked it. A triumphant smile spread across my face as I bumped the door open with my butt.

"Breakfast is served," I announced in a posh voice. I was about to set the tray down with a flourish…but was hindered by the expression on Jane's face.

Her eyes were gleaming with tears, her bottom lip quivering as she stared at a newspaper article in her hand.

"What is it?" I set the tray on the coffee table, wanting to rush around the couch to hold her.

But she held up her hand.

"Stop! Don't come near me right now."

"What's the matter?" The question came out sharp and urgent. I didn't like seeing Jane this way—particularly when I didn't know what it was about. She looked angry and heartbroken…distraught. I needed to hold her, make it better, but she wouldn't let me come near.

She sniffed and held up the paper in her hand. It flopped over before I could read the headline, but I glimpsed that wretched photo and my heart sank. I thought I'd hidden it well enough.

"I thought we said no pasts," she snapped.

"I didn't think you'd find it." I had to admit, I was a little confused. Her reaction seemed pretty extreme. After all, it was about me…not her.

"This is my story to tell!" she shouted. "I thought we were moving forward. You had no right to go and delve into this. Especially with an article that basically puts all the blame on him! This is *my* history, *my* pain. And I'll tell you about it when *I'm* ready!"

"What are you talking about?" I snatched the article off her. The bottom corner ripped, but I was too busy trying to justify myself to care. "I didn't do anything behind your back. This is *my* history, *my* pain. And I..." My voice disappeared as realization hit me like a mallet to the forehead.

Wait. Put all the blame on him?

The paper in my hand began to shake as I held it up and read the headline again.

"Tourist drivers," I whispered, my heart disintegrating to acidic ash in my stomach.

"This isn't your history!" Jane pointed at the article, her voice pitching high. "That's my...my Blake!"

Slumping against the back of the couch, I stared at the carpet, unable to look her in the eye. "My Tammy," I choked.

"What?" Jane snatched the paper and started scanning the article, her skin paling to a translucent white while her lips began to tremble. The victims weren't named in the article, as Tammy's family had yet to be informed. But all the details were accurate—the place, the time, the day...the police's theory of how it happened. Tammy was referred to as a young woman in her early twenties, and Blake had been named as the American tourist who didn't understand English road rules.

I rubbed a hand over my face, struggling to think. "You never said he died here. I thought it happened in America."

"No, we..." Her voice petered out, overtaken by rapid breathing that was turning into sobs. "This can't be happening. Are you saying that Tammy died in this accident? Was she driving the car that killed Blake?"

My head snapped up at her deep, metallic tone. Staring at her with burning eyes, I shook my head and seethed, "He was on the wrong side of the road. That's what caused the accident."

"Oh, please!" Jane dropped the article. "Everyone knows she was speeding!"

"That's not what killed her!"

"Well, it killed him!"

I stepped back from her venom and shook my head. "He was…"

"Don't," she whispered, her eyes flooding with tears. "This is a pointless argument." Closing her eyes, she turned away from me, but I could still see the tears sliding down her cheeks.

I didn't know what to say or do. Shock had frozen me to the spot. I felt numb, horrified…hazy.

Jane's silent tears morphed into whimpering sobs, but I couldn't move to comfort her. All I could think about was the fact that the guy she was supposed to marry, the one she'd been mourning for the last year, had killed Tammy. I'd spent months hating him, cursing him every time I drove that patch of road.

And now I'd gone and fallen in love with the woman he'd left behind.

With a few loud sniffs, Jane brushed past me and packed the last of her things. The zipper on her bag was loud and obnoxious as she closed her suitcase.

She didn't say goodbye, and I couldn't speak either. All I could do was stand there and watch her walk out of my life.

TWENTY-NINE

JANE

The LA streetlights glimmered beneath me. I stared out the window, my eyes sore and puffy from the constant stream of tears. My head was pounding, my body ached.

It was like losing Blake all over again. That heart-wrenching shock…that inability to think past the numb realization that the thing you loved most in the world was gone.

I knew it'd been too good to be true.

My happiness died with Blake, and then in some cruel twist of fate, I fell for the wrong man.

The plane touched down and I got out as fast as

I could.

People had been turning to check on me throughout flight, and I just wanted to be away from strangers and people who would never understand.

By the time I reached a taxi, I was a quaking mess again, tears making my belly jerk and quiver. The driver was merciful enough not to talk to me. He tried to ask me if I was okay, but I practically screamed at him that I couldn't talk about it.

He shut up after that, left me alone with my tears.

Halfway home, when I felt like I was drowning, I diverted him to Sarah's place then accidentally paid him fifty dollars extra. When he tried to call me back, I just hollered at him to keep the change. My voice was high and screechy. I barely recognized it as mine.

Stumbling down the path, I reached my best friend's front door and didn't even knock.

I just barged in.

Justin and Sarah were standing in each other's arms in their small living space, swaying to "The Luckiest." It was like a bitch slap. Blake and I used to love that song. He used to sing it to me sometimes…and now he was gone.

Killed by Harry's girlfriend.

As soon as I slammed the door shut, my friends stopped and spun to face me. Sarah's sweet smile vanished, her large eyes taking me in.

"Oh no," she whispered. "What happened?"

Sucking in a shaky breath, I steadied myself

against the back of the dining room chair. "His girlfriend killed Blake."

"What?" Sarah gasped.

"The car. She was driving the car that killed him." I covered my mouth with my hand and started ugly crying again.

Neither of them said anything. How could they? What was there to say?

Harry and I had both lost the loves of our lives because they'd killed each other. And both of us blamed the other. How could we possibly be together now?

The thought made my stomach jerk and I unleashed another loud sob, my knees buckling.

I should have hit the floor.

But I didn't.

Justin caught me under the arm and pulled me against him, wrapping his arms around me and cradling the back of my head as I pressed my forehead into his shoulder and sobbed. "Unsteady" by the X Ambassadors played in the background, covering us like a blanket.

As the chorus kicked in, Sarah's arms snaked around me too. I could feel her

THIRTY

JUSTIN

"It's So Hard To Say Goodbye" was the only sound in my room. Jason Mraz's voice wafted from my speakers—haunting and lonely.

I still couldn't feel anything. All I could do was think.

Remember.

The song made me relive Tammy's funeral. I'd carried her coffin out of the church while the song played. I'd walked past tears and whimpers, trying to stand tall against them all, already deciding to get completely plastered the second I got home. I'd had a bottle of vodka waiting.

Guilt had ravaged me, eating away at my insides until time had dulled the pain.

But sitting in my room staring at Tammy's old books and photos, my eyes darting from her smiling face to the black-and-white article that continued to destroy me...the pain felt fresh again. New and damaging.

I was grieving two women now.

The one from the past and the one who was supposed to be in my future.

"Cruel twist of fate" seemed like an understatement.

A creak on the stairs made me look up at my door. It opened with a long, slow whine to reveal Nan. The walking stick she was leaning against quivered as she laid her weight into it.

"Nan." I jumped up. "What are you doing down here? You could have fallen."

I raced over to her and guided her to the couch. She plopped into it then gave me a sad smile. "I couldn't well leave you down here on your own, drowning in your misery."

I huffed and wiped my hand under my nose then plonked back onto the floor. "I'm fine, Nan."

"That would be a lie," she muttered.

I huffed and scratched my greasy hair. "What do you want me to say?"

"Whatever you need to." Her trembling hand rested on the arm of the couch. "We all know what bottling it up does for you and I won't let you do it, Harry. You are not to go back to sleeping with all them girls and drinking your life away."

"I won't, Nan," I assured her, unwilling to admit the temptation. I'd never have called myself an alcoholic. I was able to give up the bottle with relative ease. Work had become my new drug…and then Jane.

Jane.

The name whispered through my mind, a soft, aching reminder of what I'd lost.

Nan gently prodded my knee with her walking stick. "Can I ask you something?"

I nodded without thinking.

"What's your biggest regret you've ever had? And don't answer quickly, now. I want you to really think about it."

I held my breath then let out an irritated huff. I didn't want to play her game. I didn't want to think about regrets.

She lightly tapped my foot with her walking stick, giving me a pointed look. Her hazel eyes were sharp like an eagle's, and I'd never get away with not answering.

"Uh…" I puffed out a breath. "I guess, not asking Tammy to marry me. I could have made her happy while I had her." Picking up her photo, I brushed my thumb over the dimple on her cheek and then placed the image down next to the newspaper article. I hadn't read the thing in months. If I had, would I have figured it out sooner?

"That's a pretty big regret to live with."

"It is." I nodded.

"So, why are you sitting on your arse making

another one?"

My eyes bulged as I looked up at my nan. "What?"

"You asked the pretty redhead to marry you, and now you're sitting down here listening to sad music and lamenting the loss of a girl you can never have, when a perfectly good one is waiting for you."

"She's not waiting for me, Nan. She wants nothing to do with me!"

"Is that what she said when you called her?"

"I…" With a sharp frown, I shook my head and muttered, "I can't call her."

"Why not?"

"Because her fiancé killed Tammy! Bloody idiot was driving on the wrong side of the road and she had no chance!"

"That and the speed, I suppose."

"Nan," I warned.

She huffed, her wrinkled face bunching as she tried to mirror my frown. "Don't deny the fact they were both in the wrong. It was an accident. Blaming someone's not going to change it. What does it matter now?"

My mouth fell open and I blinked at her like she'd lost one too many marbles. "Did you honestly just say that? What does it matter? Her one true love killed mine! It matters, Nan!"

"Only if you let it." She reached out, beckoning me with her fingers. I wanted to ignore them, sit on my hands and act like a stubborn five-year-old, but her kind smile bent my will.

Shuffling across the floor, I took her hand in mine. Her soft thumb rubbed the back of my hand, her voice softening to match the loving gesture. "It's your past, Harry. You can't let it dictate your future. Life is giving you a second chance. Are you really going to sit here and waste it?"

"She thinks Tammy killed—"

"Oh, stop now. We've just been through this. He was driving on the wrong side of the road without a helmet. If Tammy hadn't collided with him, someone else may well have."

"She was speeding," I croaked. "Because she was mad with me. I wouldn't marry her. I told her we had all the time in the world. She left in an angry huff, and I expected her to return and pick up where we left off...after she'd simmered down. But she never came home, Nan." My eyes burned, and I squeezed them shut to counter the tears. "I didn't want to make that same mistake again."

"Well that's because you're a smart boy. You're learning from your mistakes."

"How am I learning? I stupidly asked someone who's practically a stranger to marry me! And look where it's landed us!"

"No." Nan patted my hand and smiled. "You asked a girl who made your heart sing to marry you. Don't you see it, Harry? You've come back to life since meeting her."

"How can we make it work?" I whispered. "We have this huge chasm between us now. Life's not fair, Nan."

"Life is life, child. Sometimes it tries to kill you,

and other times it offers you gifts you don't even understand." Her voice was husky and fierce. "You both lost and somehow you've been brought together...to be with each other. To fill that gaping hole left behind. Don't be a coward and turn your back on this."

I winced and looked away from her loving, wrinkled face. "She won't want me now. It's too hard."

"No!" She squeezed my hand, tighter than I thought she'd be able to. "It's just a fight...and one you can win."

I gazed up at her determined expression. Her eyes shone with conviction.

"You just need to decide if she's worth it."

THIRTY-ONE

JANE

I wandered from the basketball courts across to the fields. Tuesday lunch duty was my least favorite time of the week. I felt bad for not loving it more. It was a great chance to interact with the students on a casual, friendly basis, but it never seemed to work out that way. They were all busy hanging out with their friends, and they weren't about to stop what they were doing to come over and chat with me.

And so duty became a time of monitoring the odd scuffle, telling off a few students here and there, but mainly watching a school full of tweens develop into young adults.

The worst part about it was having so much time to think. Because I wasn't distracted by grading, teaching, or conversation with my colleagues, my mind could wander wherever it liked, and that particular week it was obsessed with Harry.

It'd been over a week since the shocking revelation, and I still felt drained and haunted by it. I kept having these horrible dreams, imagining how the crash went down. Inevitably I'd wake up in a cold sweat, panting and crying, scraping my fingers through my hair and begging the nightmare away.

The thump of a basketball made me turn, and I blocked the orange bullet in the nick of time.

"Sorry, Miss Buford!" Reese gripped the fence with a grimace.

I picked up the ball and threw it back. "No problem."

He caught it, smiled at me, and then dribbled the ball back into the game. I headed for the soccer field, sticking with my usual figure-eight route around my designated area.

Rubbing my eye, I readjusted my shades and lamented how tired I felt. The combination of nightmares and crying exhausted me. I never did well without enough sleep. I was trying to throw all my energy into work, but that only left me further depleted. Grading papers was hardly inspiring.

The soccer fields were busy with their usual

swarm of boys and girls. I scanned the moving bodies, making sure everyone was in bounds and doing what they were supposed to. The game to my right looked like a coed match filled with shouts, laughter, and an excessive amount of flirting between Carson and Ruby. I couldn't help a small grin as I watched her make an unnecessary tackle, just so she'd have an excuse to touch his shoulder.

By the look on his face, he didn't seem to mind.

Glancing to my left, I checked out the more serious game between a group of eighth-grade boys. A line of giggling girls was sitting on the grass, pulling out blades and tearing them in half while they subtly watched the boys play. More eye-flirting. I couldn't help shaking my head.

Kids going through puberty were just starting to figure themselves out, become aware of their sexuality and how they felt about the whole *falling in love* thing. It was a privilege to watch, and one of the reasons I chose to teach middle school students.

I just never thought it would hurt so much.

Because I never thought my love would be stolen so swiftly...twice.

I grimaced and turned from the field, heading into the quiet corridors of Block C to make sure no kids were inside where they shouldn't be.

My phone started ringing the second I opened the door. I pulled it from my pocket, my tapping heels coming to a stop as I read the name on the screen.

"Harry," I whispered and sucked in a breath.

Did I ignore it?

My brain said yes but my thumb said no. It swiped across the screen, and I lifted the phone to my ear.

"Hello, Harry."

"Hi." His voice was husky...quiet.

Tears stung my eyes. I blinked and scanned the corridor, not sure where to look. "Why are you calling me?"

"Because I miss you."

The conviction with which he said the words made my nose tingle. My lips wobbled, and I pressed my finger into the corner of my eye to stop myself from crying.

"I'm sorry I let you walk out, and I'm sorry I haven't called sooner. I was just in shock."

I started walking, looking into the first classroom as I passed. "You shouldn't be calling me, Harry."

"Why?"

"You know why! This can't work."

"Maybe it can."

"Harry, come on. You think my first love killed yours. I think the same about you! It's a black cloud over us and it will always be there."

"Only if we let it."

"As soon as we get irritated with each other it'll rear its ugly head. We may survive for a while, but it will ultimately break us."

"No, it doesn't have to be like that. It's all about perspective. I can change my thinking. I'm willing to do whatever I have to. Whatever it takes."

"Please, don't." I stopped at the next door, sucking in a breath. I noticed it was ajar, so I rested my hand on the door handle, needing to wrap up the call and pull myself together before the bell rang. "I have to go."

"No, Jane, please."

"I can't do this right now. In fact, I don't know if I ever can. My heart barely survived losing Blake. I can't lose you too."

"Then stop pushing me away."

I shook my head. "I have to let go now or it'll only get worse."

"Jane, please." His voice was stretched tight with desperation, and I could feel myself crumbling. I missed him too. Ached for what we had in Europe…and then when he stayed. I'd been so happy, started to believe that I could love again.

And then I found that article and it all fell apart. I had to take the warning for what it was. I was not meant to love again.

"Goodbye, Harry," I whimpered into the phone, then hung up before he could respond.

He called straight back, but I ignored it and turned off my phone altogether. Covering my mouth, I gazed at the screen, tears trickling down my cheeks as I tried to reassure myself that I was doing the right thing.

"Are you okay, Miss B?"

I gasped as the door creaked open. Gazing down at Brandy, I thought about telling her off for being in a restricted area. Students weren't allowed inside on a sunny day. But staring into those big brown eyes of hers, all I could do was droop my shoulders and mutter, "Life's just…"

"Shit?"

"Yeah." I nodded, fresh tears flooding my vision. I swiped them away and noticed her smile.

It was soft and tender. Grabbing my hand, she led me into the science room and guided me to the stool next to hers. Drawings covered the lab table along with a strewn pencil case. Her iPad was beside her, quietly playing music. It was so soft I could barely hear it, but then I recognized the guitar riff and voice—"Say" by John Mayer.

A great song and no doubt perfect for drawing to. Glancing at the image closest to me, I had to smile at the beautiful white unicorn with a silver and purple mane. It was stunning and drawn with Disney-quality potential.

I gave her an impressed smile. She beamed and sat on the stool in front of me.

"You know you're not supposed to be in here, right?" I tried to give her a reprimanding look, but it disintegrated the second she explained why she was breaking the rules.

"I can't think straight with all the noise outside, and no one really understands why I have to do this."

Running my finger along a royal blue pencil, I rolled it back and forth across the lab table, thinking of Harry and the way he'd spoken to Brandy.

How much she'd softened since that short conversation. She was leaving for Chile in just over

MELISSA PEARL

a week. I was going to miss her.

Picking up an olive green pencil, she started shading a tree. "Want to talk about it?"

"No." My voice sounded so lifeless.

I didn't want to go back to being that person again.

But I didn't want to have to dredge up my life list either.

Everything just seemed like hard work. My shattered heart, which I'd somehow managed to glue back together, felt fragile again, on the brink of total decimation.

Opening her sketchpad, Brandy ripped out a fresh sheet of paper and placed it down in front of me. "Draw it. I swear it works."

Her kind smile was doing a number on me. When her surly face had appeared in my doorway at the beginning of the year, I was worried I'd never grow to like her.

But she'd really opened up, somehow accepted her parents' divorce and the impending departure. I wished I could have adapted that easily.

"Go on, Miss B. Draw." She tapped my paper.

After a reluctant pause, I picked up the blue pencil and started with a swirl in the middle of my page that soon became a thick question mark, dominating the sheet of paper.

Was Harry right?

Could we overcome this barrier between us?

Could we let it go and move forward together?

The bell rang, making me flinch. Brandy gasped and started gathering up her belongings, shoving

232

the loose sheets into her sketchbook and jamming the pencils and sharpener into her case.

I held out the blue pencil, but she shook her head with a lopsided grin. "You keep it."

"I'll give it back to you before you leave."

"Okay." She nodded then rushed out the door.

The corridor started to fill, the noise rising in a swift crescendo. I had to get back to my classroom, but I wasn't ready to move. I just kept staring at that question mark and wondering.

Could I do it?

My forehead wrinkled, and I wrote over the top of my question mark in capital letters... *TOO HARD!!*

Scrunching the paper in my fist, I walked to the trash and threw it out before entering the busy corridor and trying to get into the right headspace to teach a fifty-minute English class... and get over Harry Tindal.

THIRTY-TWO

HARRY

"See You Someday" was torturing me as I ran along the edge of the cliff. I looked out across the ocean, the morning sun only just breaching the horizon. The dark mass of sea was growing light at the edges while the sky turned a pale peach color. I'd left in the dark and I'd planned to return the same way, but my jog took me off my usual course and I ended up on the cliffs, running through the cool morning grass and trying to escape the emotions coursing through me.

My music choices were of no help at all, but shuffle play seemed determined to pick every melancholy love song Tammy had added to our playlists when we first set up our Spotify account. I should have switched the damn thing off and run in silence, but for some sick reason, I was compelled to listen to them.

Sweat poured from my hairline as I raced up the hill to the lone tree that sat along the path. I'd walked past it so many times before. Tammy and I used to picnic beside it in the summer. When I reached it, I stopped to catch my breath, resting my hand on the trunk and sucking in lungfuls of air.

I hadn't run that far in a long time. My body was complaining bitterly.

Please don't do this to us, Harry. First the liquor and the sex, then the work. Are we now falling into a running phase? God help us.

My tired muscles whined as I leaned against the tree, gazing out at the vast ocean and wondering what it'd feel like to just run and jump into it.

The fall would kill me, but imagine the sheer ecstasy…the thrill before I hit the water.

Drooping my head, I concentrated on the beads of sweat running down my cheeks. I'd never be able to do it. I couldn't take my own life.

So what the hell was I supposed to do with it?

When Tammy died, I figured I'd just find a way to survive…and I did.

But then I met Jane and she showed me how to live again.

And that's what I wanted.

To live.

With her.

Pushing off the tree, I got ready to start running but was hindered by a heart-shaped carving I'd never noticed before. Running my finger into the grooves, my heart hiccupped to a stop then took off.

"Jane plus Blake. One thousand years," I murmured, still tracing the letters.

My Jane.

His Jane.

"Is that how long you expected to love her, mate?" I looked up at the branches above me. The leaves were starting to yellow for the autumn. Soon the tree would be standing bare, watching over the cliffs like a winter soldier.

I wondered if Jane had seen it. I had to assume Blake carved it. No doubt a romantic gesture before they got married.

Digging my fingers into the trunk, I let myself relive that day from Jane's perspective. Since she'd fled my house I'd researched her story, and I could only imagine the horror of finding out that her groom was lying dead on the roadside while she waited for him in her wedding dress.

It was no wonder she was so afraid to let me in.

The fact she'd even let me near made me admire her so much.

I thought of her loneliness. That desolation that I understood so well.

I would never forget returning home to our little flat and the oppressive silence that followed me into every room. I'd tried to fill it with music, women, parties…but it'd never worked. The aching loneliness plagued me until I moved out and in with my nan.

Living with a loved one softened the blow.

Living with Jane revived me again.

And it revived her too.

I checked my watch and calculated the time. It'd be eleven p.m. in LA. She'd be lying in her bed, all alone in her quiet little apartment.

Impulse pulled the phone from my running belt, and I pressed her name before I could think better of it.

I waited three rings before a voice I didn't expect answered, "Hello, Harry."

"Uh, Jane?" I frowned.

"No, it's Sarah."

"Oh, hi. Um, I'm sorry to call so late."

"That's all right. Jane's in the shower. She wasn't answering her phone, and I just had to pop in to see if she was okay."

"Is she?" My eyes stung. I wanted to be there. I didn't want Jane to be worried, anxious…not answering her phone. I wanted her to be happy again.

"She was making pretty good headway through her second bottle of Merlot, so I'm glad I stopped by."

I closed my eyes and shuddered. "I can't…do this."

"Do what?"

"Just stand back while she suffers."

Sarah didn't say anything at first. Then after a soft breath, she murmured, "How are you holding up?"

Running a hand through my sweaty curls, I gazed at the peachy sky. "It's been a shock."

"I couldn't believe it. At first Justin and I just didn't know what to say. We couldn't talk about it for like a week, but the more time passes, the more we wonder if…"

"If what?"

"Do you love her, Harry? Even in spite of what you've found out."

"Of course I do. I don't blame her for Tammy's death. I can't even blame Blake anymore. It was an accident, and if it had never happened, I never would've experienced what I have with Jane. I'd still be cruising along, pissing off my girlfriend and trying to avoid any conversation that involved the words love or commitment." I winced. "Please, don't get me wrong. I wish Tammy had never died, and I of course wish the same for Blake, but the truth is, they have…and somehow life has sought to bring Jane and me together. I can't help feeling like maybe it's a sign that we're destined."

Another pause that made me hold my breath.

Then Sarah softly snickered. "You're a good man, Harry Tindal."

I smiled sadly at the sunrise. "Do you think she'll ever be able to move past it? When I spoke to her a couple of days ago, she seemed rather adamant."

"I think she's just shocked and scared. She was nervous enough falling for you, and this is like a slap in the face. She's right back to where she was after Blake died, worried about her future and getting hurt again."

"I understand." I tucked my hand beneath my armpit and leaned against the tree. "I guess I just have to give her time."

Sarah scoffed. "I don't know. Jane has the ability to be extremely stubborn."

"If only I could see her. It's impossible doing this kind of thing over the phone."

"So why don't you come?"

"I can't just show up on her doorstep. I don't want to upset her."

"Sometimes you have to take a leap of faith, Harry. If she chooses not to jump with you then so be it, but you have to give her the chance."

My chest expanded with a hopeful breath, and I stood tall and nodded. "All right."

"Okay, then." Her voice sounded brighter, like she was sitting straight and smiling.

"Well, I guess I'll get going."

"Keep me posted on your plans. I'll do what I can from my end."

"Thank you, Sarah."

We said our goodbyes, and once I'd hung up the phone, I just stood there staring across the ocean. Did I do it? Did I spend my last few pennies crossing an ocean so I could tell Jane I'd move past this mountain for her...that I loved her no matter what?

It was a risk. The chances of her shaking her head were bloody high.

Slowly turning back for home, I lost the

willpower to run, instead trudging through the grass while I thought it through. The early morning light was touching my back, pushing me home when the phone in my hand started ringing. Glancing at the screen, I felt my breath hitch.

I wasn't sure if I wanted to answer or not. What if it was a warning not to come...a swift rebuttal before I spent the last of my funds?

Clenching my jaw, I prepped my argument and cautiously raised the phone to my ear.

THIRTY-THREE

JANE

The shower was scalding, just the way I needed it to be. I stayed in far too long, hoping Sarah would be gone by the time I got out. It had been so sweet of her to pop in and check on me, but it was so late. I was exhausted and I didn't feel like *talking it through*. Besides, my head was still kind of spinning from the wine, and although the shower had helped to clear it, I didn't think I was up for any kind of coherent conversation.

Switching off the spray, I let the drips slowly run down my body before snapping out of my stupor and reaching for a towel.

Soft music was still playing from my speakers in the kitchen and I sighed. Sarah was obviously still there, waiting to tuck me in like a mother hen.

I took my time drying off, and when I finally exited my poky bathroom it was nearly midnight. I paused in the doorway and scanned the apartment.

"Sarah?"

Peeking around the fridge, I gazed at my speakers and realized she was gone. It was a relief…albeit a lonely one.

"You Matter To Me" filtered through the apartment, only adding to my silent despair. The beautiful duet didn't fit into my life. It couldn't.

I wouldn't let myself matter to anybody again.

The thought sliced through me, brutal and swift.

Did I really want to be that way?

"I have to!" I shouted. "I can't do this anymore!"

Sucking in a breath, I pressed the towel against my lips and fought the tears. No more. I couldn't cry or think or feel anymore.

So where did that leave me?

Robot mode.

I promised myself I wouldn't go there either.

"This is too hard!" I yelled at the ceiling. "How can I be with someone who killed…" I bit my lips together then shuffled across to my bed, flicking the curtain aside and flopping onto the mattress. "He didn't kill anybody," I whispered. "Blake killed himself." My eyes snapped back to the ceiling, my voice hard and bitter. "Didn't you? No helmet! What were you thinking?" I screamed and thumped the bed, crying out in hopeless frustration. "You selfish bastard! How could you leave me on our frickin' wedding day!" I let out another scream and pounded my fist against the mattress until I was a panting, exhausted mess.

I'd never let myself get angry with Blake. I'd always made him the victim, directing all my venom at the speeding driver…Harry's sweetheart.

The thought crushed me all over again and I curled onto my side, clutching my knees. "I miss you so much," I whispered to Blake. "But now I miss him too…and it hurts. I don't want to hurt anymore."

The song shifted to "Marry Me" by Train. I closed my eyes, fresh tears burning me. It was a cruel joke. A song so beautiful was a punch in the face.

Struggling off the bed, I kicked the curtain aside, ready to storm across the room and kill the music, but I ended up catching my foot in the fine netting and tearing it. I let out a hopeless whimper as I fingered the gaping hole, then growled and fisted the fragile material. It tore easily and was soon lying on the floor in a sad, pathetic heap. Just like me—broken, torn, lifeless.

Kicking the fabric aside, I marched to my phone, set on switching off the music. I snatched it up and pressed pause, then noticed a text from Sarah.

Sorry I had to split. Something's come up. Check your email.

I was too tired to check my email, but curiosity got the better of me and I opened my inbox right away.

Sarah's address popped up and I opened her message.

Sorry I had to take off. I'm working with an overseas client and it's turning out to be a big ordeal!

Anyway, I know you're hurting right now and I know you're confused. But as a friend who can step back and see things with a little more perspective, I just want to say that you should trust your heart on this one. Stop worrying about the future and embrace the now. Be the Jane Harry taught you how to be. Whether you take him back or not almost doesn't matter. When you left for England in July, you were on a mission to find yourself, to figure out how to live again. And you did that. Don't let this roadblock stop you from taking a chance at life. Be brave. Keep jumping down rabbit holes and see where they take you.

Love you always, my precious friend,
Sparks

I stared at the message until my eyes lost focus.

"Jump down rabbit holes," I grumped. "Is she kidding? I'm not after an Alice adventure. I just want..." I sighed. I didn't know. What did I really want?

To feel safe again.

To be happy.

Dropping the phone on the table, I shuffled back to my exposed bed. I flicked off the lights, crawled beneath the covers, and pulled them up to my chin. My little apartment was drenched in darkness and quiet. I used to find this time of night so peaceful, but it'd become a torment. Sliding my hand across the empty sheets beside me, I lamented the fact it was empty, cried for the fact I didn't have the courage to call Harry and ask him to be mine again.

I didn't want to see where that rabbit hole led. I just wanted to stop crying and figure out how to live like a normal person.

*****

The days continued like they always did. Life moved on.

Breakfast was eaten. Classes were taught. Papers were graded, and my students neared the weekend with growing agitation. It was always that way. Thursdays and Fridays were my most challenging.

Checking my planner, I quickly went over what I wanted to achieve by the end of the day. Part of me wanted to scrap it and just play games, but I had assessments we were working toward, and with Thanksgiving less than a month away, I couldn't really slack off.

The morning bell was due to ring in half an hour. I had my music playing while I prepped, but I could still hear the early morning bustle outside. Teachers and students were already arriving.

I doubted any of them would disturb me. With the anti-social vibes I'd been generating lately, I figured I'd be left alone...which was why I was so surprised when my door clicked open.

I spun from the whiteboard, my lips parting as I

spotted my visitor.

"Aren't you supposed to be at the airport?"

Brandy's smile was sad yet accepting. "We're leaving in a couple of minutes. Dad's driving us."

"Wow, okay." My eyebrows shot up in surprise.

"I know. Hopefully he can keep it together. Mom and him had good chats last night and she gave in, said he could see us off."

"How do you feel about that?"

"Good." She nodded, her smile growing genuine. "I, um...think we're in a good place. He's gonna come visit for Thanksgiving and Mom said I could come up for Christmas."

I smiled. "Well, that's really positive."

Brandy shuffled further into the room, closing the door behind her. "I, um, wanted to give you something." She held out a small handmade notebook. "Actually, it's not for you. It's for that guy who told me to draw how I felt."

"Harry," I whispered.

"Yeah, him."

My hands quivered as I took the book from her. If she noticed, she didn't say anything.

The cover was a stunning drawing of three dragons. The daddy dragon was blue, Mom was red, and the baby was a stunning purple.

The Way I Want It by Brandy Hiseman.

Brushing my hand over the cover, I gave the book, then Brandy, a watery smile. "This is amazing. You're a talented girl."

"That's what Dad said." She blushed. "I gave him a copy last night. I think he really liked it."

"May I?" I went to open the cover.

"Of course."

Flicking through the pages, I skimmed the unfolding story. From the happy beginning surrounded in pulsing red hearts to the dragon fight in the middle where the hearts lay shattered in pieces on the dry earth. The next page the baby dragon was crying. Her tears then turned into a waterfall, which became a river that made the grass grow and created a flower-covered meadow where three dragons rested in the sun, peaceful smiles on their reptile-like faces. The blue and red dragons were no longer sitting together, but the purple dragon sat between them, touching them with her outspread wings. A big heart mended with stitches shone above them like a sun.

"I don't think it's enough to get them back together, but Dad said he's going to try really hard to stop yelling, and Mom said she's going to respect him because he's my father and she loves me."

Her genuine smile made my chest swell with pride.

"You are such a brave kid, and you're going to do really great."

She shrugged, letting out a nervous titter. "Dad said I can keep sending him photos of my drawings, and then he gave me an iPhone so we can keep in touch."

"Score." I grinned.

"I know, right?" She giggled then bit the edge of her lip, her eyes shimmering with tears. "I'm still scared to leave, but Mom says it'll be a new adventure and those always make us stronger. I just have to have faith."

Dropping the booklet, I came around the desk and wrapped my arms around Brandy, holding her against me as she softly cried. "You're gonna do just fine. I believe in you."

She squeezed back. "I believe in you too, Miss B."

Pulling away from me, she gazed up at my face, her eyes glimmering. "Thanks for everything. And tell Harry he's the best. I'm so grateful that he came into my life, even for just a minute. He made everything better."

I couldn't respond. My throat was too clogged with emotion, so I just bobbed my head and forced a smile.

Satisfied, she ran for the door and gave me one last wave before disappearing into the corridor. With slow, numb feet, I walked to my desk and picked up the booklet again.

Like some kind of sign, "It's Good" started playing on my stereo. I went still, letting the words soak into me. Tears welled in my eyes and I hugged the book to my chest, my thoughts consumed by only one thing...

Harry.

My door creaked open again, and I jumped when Principal Rogers cleared his throat.

"Oh, sorry. I didn't mean to startle you."

I let out a breathy laugh and waved my hand, jumping over to my stereo and killing the song that was trying to change my mind.

Placing Brandy's book down beside it, I forced a smile and turned to him.

"What's up, William?"

His shoes sounded loud on the shiny floor as he crossed the room. Reaching into his jacket pocket, he pulled out an envelope while saying, "I've arranged cover for you today, tomorrow, and Monday. There's somewhere I need you to be."

"Really?" I took the envelope, my frown only deepening when I read the message on the outside.

Bombs away.

I immediately thought of Harry and wondered if the mystery envelope was from him. But I recognized Sarah's handwriting. I tried to ignore the wave of disappointment cresting through me. A surprise from my bestie was a safer bet anyway.

Ripping it open, I pulled out the sheets of paper and carefully unfolded them. The top page was a handwritten note.

It's time to jump down a rabbit hole.
Love you xx
Sparks

With trembling fingers, I checked the pages below and found an e-ticket for Antigua and a brochure for a luxury resort on a private island. I flicked open the glossy pamphlet, blinking stupidly at the pictures while my brain tried to catch up with what the hell was going on.

William cleared his throat again, checking his

watch quite obviously. "Apparently your best friend thinks you need a girls' weekend of luxury to talk some sense into you. I'm not exactly clear on what sense needs to be spoken, but your mother is waiting for you at the front entrance with a bag of clothes and your passport."

My mouth dropped open a little wider. "I can't just leave work."

"Why not? You're all planned, and a substitute teacher's been arranged. You have no excuse to stay." He gave me a wry smile. "And your friend, Sarah, was very compelling on the phone."

"But..." I lifted the pages. "How is this happening?"

The middle-aged man's eyes softened with a kind smile as he approached me and gently held my shoulders. "Jane, you're one of my best teachers. You work harder than any other staff member at this school. In all honesty, it worried me...until you returned from your summer break with a new lease of life." Stepping back, his lips turned into a sad smile. "But you're slipping back into your old ways. I've watched the light fade from your eyes...so I think giving you a few days to go and relax on a beach with your best friend can only be a good thing."

"But..."

"You need to clear your head. Everyone who cares about you thinks so." His smile told me he was on that list. "Now, go." He stepped aside and pointed at the door.

I still couldn't quite believe him and just stood

there until he started gathering my things.

"If you don't get moving, you'll miss your flight." He held out my computer bag.

Taking Brandy's booklet, I slipped it in the side pocket and hitched the strap over my shoulder. "Are you honestly letting me leave five minutes before first bell?"

"Like I said, your friend was very compelling." He winked and walked to the door, opening it wide and encouraging me through.

I blinked a couple of times then shook my head before murmuring, "Bombs away" and heading out to meet my mother.

THIRTY-FOUR

HARRY

My father fidgeted with his keys while he stood beside me at the airport. I'd already checked in my bag and was anxiously waiting for my flight time. I'd say goodbye to my old man and head through security then hopefully on to something wonderful.

Doubts scoured my insides, leaving me raw and tender. Gripping my Starbucks venti cup, I took another sip only to find it empty. I walked away from my twitching father and threw the cup into the recycling bin. I should never have asked him to drive me up. When I'd told the family my intentions, my sister had swooned and hugged me.

Mum and Nan were on board, but Dad didn't say anything. Unfortunately, he'd been the only family member available to drive me to Heathrow. Our trip had been a quiet one.

Walking back to his side, I hitched my computer bag on my shoulder and considered saying a quick goodbye, but something held me back. Maybe it was the fact I was trying to live a regret-free life, I'm not sure. But instead of doing our standard no-nonsense goodbye, I decided to make my dad spit out whatever he was holding in.

Pointing at the security checkpoint, I glanced at Dad and said, "I'm walking through that gate in ten minutes, so whatever it is you're thinking right now, you better hurry up and say it."

He slipped his keys into his pocket and sighed. "You sure about this, son? You haven't even called to tell her you're coming."

"If I do that, she'll tell me not to. I need an element of surprise if this is going to work."

With a dubious smile, he scratched his whiskers and nodded.

"I know you think I'm reckless and impulsive, but you can't think I'm all bad if you're lending me the money to pull this off, right?"

His head kept bobbing. "Your mother would have my hide if I hadn't."

I grinned. "She's a good woman."

Dad's lips bunched, his round cheeks puffing out like he was fighting the words inside him.

"What, Dad? Just say it."

"Marriage can be tough. I thought it'd be this

fun adventure, see, and then it turned into a hard slog and I just couldn't do it anymore."

"Was leaving Mum the biggest regret of your life?"

After a pause, he gave me a slow nod then shrugged. "I had to do it. I had to walk away in order to realize how much I loved her."

"You took a bloody long time to figure it out," I muttered, unable to keep the bitterness from my tone.

"I know I did wrong by you kids. I hurt you."

I scoffed and shook my head. "You know, you're the reason I didn't want to marry Tammy. I didn't want to promise her something and then not deliver. Even though I was sure I could love her for the rest of my life, I was still too scared to go through with it—" I poked Dad lightly in the shoulder. "—because of you."

Dad's expression flooded with regret, his eyes begging for forgiveness as he blinked at me.

"But I'm not letting you hold me back anymore. I love Jane. I want to be with her. I *want* to be her husband."

Dad took a minute to speak. I decided to wait it out. This was the first deep and meaningful we'd really had, and I couldn't be a heartless bastard and simply walk away from it.

Finally he found the ability to choke out, "I never should have left the family. It was selfish and although I figured out who I really was, I ended up destroying something beautiful in order to do it. I was always glad you never married Tammy. I was worried you'd make the same mistakes I did."

"I lost her because I was worried I'd make the same mistakes you did."

His apologetic smile was weak and fleeting.

"I'm not going to lose Jane. I know who I am. I know what I want. This may seem impulsive, but if Tammy's death has taught me anything, it's that you can't count on getting a tomorrow, so I have to make the most of today. I love Jane. She's meant to be mine. Look at all the circumstances surrounding it. You can't deny that fate has brought us together. I have to convince her that's true."

"You might get fifty years of tomorrows, Harry. Life isn't always a trip through Europe and romantic dinners by the beach. Sometimes it's bills and housework…the boring stuff. Do you think you can love her through that too?"

"Being with her, no matter what we're doing, makes me happy. It's as easy as breathing."

The wrinkles around Dad's eyes deepened when he smiled at me. "I know that feeling. I wish I'd realized how precious it was when I had it. I wish I'd figured out that love—slow and comfortable is the best kind there is. If you think you can love Jane for a lifetime, then I'll support you."

My lips tipped into a sad smile. "We can't guarantee life, Dad. But I can tell you that I will love Jane every day I'm given, and I'll love her with everything I have."

Dad lost his voice as he stared at me, his eyes shining with pride. Lurching forward, he wrapped me in his arms and patted my back. "You tell her just that, son."

"I will, Dad."

We pounded each other a couple more times on the shoulders then pulled apart. After one more meaningful smile, I stepped away from him and turned for the security checkpoint.

It was time to go and win back my girl.

All I could hope was that she'd be willing to listen.

THIRTY-FIVE

JANE

I tried to relax on the plane, I really did. But I could barely eat a mouthful of food, and I figured turning up completely drunk to see Sarah wouldn't fly. So I just stared out my window, worrying that I was making a huge mistake.

Did I really want an excuse to think some more?

Sarah loved surprises, and the idea of whisking me off for a girly weekend no doubt thrilled her. But I wasn't in the frame of mind to hang out, shoot the breeze…chat about Harry and what I was supposed to do.

It wouldn't be possible to lie on some exotic

beach and relax, not when my heart and mind were in torment. Running my hand over the cover of Brandy's book, I gazed at the sweet purple dragon and couldn't help a soft smile.

Harry awakened that in her.

Just like he'd awakened life in me.

I missed him.

The closer I got to Antigua, the more I realized that I wanted to be on that island with *him*, experiencing all it had to offer. Sarah too, of course—I mean, she was my bestie—but Harry just brought everything to life.

So what the hell was I so afraid of?

Thumping my head back with a sigh, I closed my eyes and willed my brain to stop working.

Thinking hurt.

Living hurt.

*****

The sun was piping hot on my skin as I walked down the steps and onto the tarmac at the small airport. I was going to burn like a French fry if I wasn't careful. Tugging my long-sleeve shirt out of the top of my bag, I stopped and pulled it on, covering my pale skin until I could slather on the sunscreen.

Pushing up my shades, I squinted to the building ahead and noticed Sarah running out the doors to greet me. She jumped up and down, waving wildly and grinning like a cheerleader.

I had to laugh.

She was right to be this happy.

We hadn't done anything so girly and BFF-ish since before her wedding. It was time to remedy that.

Running forward, I wrapped my arms around her and spoke into her ear. "You are crazy. Dragging me away from home with this big surprise. What are you up to?"

She pulled out of my embrace. "Nothing! I just felt like you had to get away, and I couldn't resist my awesome rabbit hole metaphor. Come on, surprises are fun!"

I made a face and she laughed at me, threading her arm around mine. "One of my clients has a wedding here this weekend, and I just thought it'd be the perfect chance for you to get away. Your mom agreed with me and paid for your ticket. I got you the room for free." She winked.

"This is unbelievable," I murmured.

She squeezed my arm and rested her cheek on my shoulder. "You need this, Jane. You need to get out of your own space so you can think clearly. No work distractions, no sad little apartment to wallow in." Spreading her arm wide, she sniffed the air then sighed. "Beautiful fresh air, stunning blue sky. It's the perfect place to center yourself and figure out what you want."

I forced a nod.

Man, I was exhausted. The idea of centering myself felt impossible. I'd been running on empty since returning from England, and the flight to Antigua wasn't helping.

But holy cow it was beautiful.

As I walked out of the airport and headed for the docks, I couldn't help looking around me, smelling that salty sea air, gazing at the stunning palm trees against the blue sky backdrop. Whoever was getting married in this place was insanely lucky. An amazing choice for the couple...if they both made it to the altar.

I swallowed and closed my eyes against visions from my wedding day. They weren't as forceful as they once were, but they still stung and lashed my already tender wounds. It was enough to put me off marriage for life.

Funny how that thought hurt too.

Harry's impulsive proposal whistled through my mind as I boarded the boat. A fist squeezed my heart to a mushy pulp when I remembered walking into that pub and saying yes, imagining we'd have a life together.

I thumped onto the wooden bench, clutching my bag strap and blinking rapidly.

"You okay?" Sarah touched my arm.

I nodded then went for a quick distraction so she wouldn't look too closely at my locked jaw and flaring nostrils. "Justin here?"

Sarah shook her head but didn't look at me when she answered. "No, he's holding up the fort back home. We've got another wedding next weekend, which he's doing last-minute details for." She whipped back to face me, a bright smile on her lips. "Besides, I didn't want him getting in our way." She winked then squeezed my knee when I didn't smile back. "This is going to be good for you. It's a private island with only wedding guests, so it won't be overcrowded. I do have to work, but when I'm free we can grab a glass of wine and go find a quiet place to hang, and when I'm busy you can just enjoy the luxury of the resort."

I forced a tight smile.

Gazing out across the ocean, I focused on the sound of the waves hitting the boat, the bump and sway as we made our way to the small island. The water was a vibrant turquoise, so clear I could see my toes if I dunked them in.

Just like the water Harry and I had jumped into.

The memory was so crystal clear in my mind. His funny muscle-man poses, comparing himself to a demigod and then softly calling me Aphrodite.

My eyes burned and I turned away from my friend. The wind ruffled tendrils of hair against my cheek. I tucked them behind my ear to stop the tickle.

Sarah told me all about the resort as we went, no doubt trying to fuel my enthusiasm.

By the time we pulled into the shore, she'd wrapped up her sales pitch and I was grateful for it. She was making the place sound a little too magical and I was wise enough to know that magic didn't exist…not in my life anyway.

"Welcome to Jumby Bay!" A gorgeous attendant with dark eyes and a white smile helped me off the boat.

I let go of his hand and walked down the pier toward the luxury white buildings with their orange tiled roofs. Perfectly cut lawn, bordered with palm trees, paved the way to a pristine white villa that was obviously the reception and restaurant area. Rooms must have been on the second floor, and I wondered which one I'd be sharing with Sarah. I assumed we were sharing; how else would she get me the room for free?

"We don't need to worry about checking you in. I've already got the room organized." Sarah grinned, then asked the valet to take my bags. "Why don't you follow him and go freshen up. I'll join you shortly. I just need to check in with the manager about a quick wedding thing."

"Okay." I nodded and followed the porter, gazing around me as I went.

He placed the bag Mom packed for me into the back of a golf cart and indicated for me to sit. It was hard to resist his friendly smile, and I gave him a polite grin as I sat down beside him.

Thankfully he didn't try to strike up any conversation. Instead he hummed as we drove around the curving pathway. Lush vegetation that had been tamed by expert gardeners grew on my right while the vast ocean lapped against the rocks on our left. The salty breeze cooled my skin, urging me to relax. Tucking my bangs behind my ear, I adjusted my shades and willed myself to listen.

I couldn't come somewhere this beautiful only to be consumed by sadness. If I was going to think straight, I did need to relax.

The cart stopped outside a luxurious villa and I gave the porter a bemused frown. "Here?"

"Yes, here." He grinned, the smile taking over his face.

Jumping out, he grabbed my bags, and I followed him up the path to a place that looked like it was reserved for celebrity guests. I was surprised they'd put Sarah up in such flashy accommodation. I supposed she *was* organizing their big event. It made me wonder how amazing the couple's villa must be.

The porter opened the door, and I was expecting to walk into a cacophony of wedding gear—a table covered with centerpieces, bridesmaids' dresses, and shoes neatly lined up for the day. Possibly a lavish wedding gown she'd made.

But when the porter ushered me inside, all I saw was a pristine villa. Beautiful cane couches with plump white cushions and turquoise throw pillows sat in a U-shape on the large beige tiles. The bifold doors were open, giving me a view of palm trees and sparkling ocean. Dividing the villa from the beach was a gorgeous swimming pool surrounded by comfy-looking deck chairs.

I gaped at the porter, who just kept smiling as he placed my bag in the bedroom. With a polite nod, he excused himself and left me to get settled.

It took me a few moments to move. I was still too stunned by what Sarah had arranged for me.

Sliding off my long-sleeve shirt, I folded it as I walked into the bedroom, figuring I should probably open up my bag and find out what my mother had actually packed.

But as I walked into the room, I spotted

something on the bed that made me jerk to a stop.

In the middle of the navy blue duvet, about a foot down from the mountain of plump pillows, was a small ring box. The lid was open...and inside was a diamond ring that had an old *passed down through the generations* kind of look about it.

I gasped. My first thought was that the porter must have accidentally dropped me at the bridal suite. Humiliation swept through me and I was about to grab my bag and run to find Sarah when someone stepped out from hiding and whispered, "Hello, Jane."

My eyes glassed with instant tears as I gazed across the room at Harry.

He was dressed in slacks and a rumpled shirt. His hair was a mess, his face peppered with light stubble. But his eyes froze me. They drank me in, sparkling with affection as a slow smile drew out his lips.

"Wh..." I breathed then pointed to the ring on the bed then back to him. "Wha...?"

His snicker was soft as he scratched the back of his neck and inched to the edge of the bed. "I know you told me this was too hard, but I just had to see you. I had to give this one more chance. So, please, if you could just hear me out...and then if you still don't want to...I'll go."

I rubbed my forehead. "Does Sarah know—?"

"It was her idea."

"Right." I crossed my arms and glanced at the ring again. My heart was throbbing in my chest, pounding through my head and making it hard to hear.

I closed my eyes and drew in a breath. As soon as they popped back open, Harry started talking, his voice husky and earnest.

"I know you're scared, and I am too. I know our histories are connected in this horrible way, and I wish you'd never had to face that, Jane. But the truth is, it's in the past. We were wrong to hide it from each other, but maybe it was fate. If we'd known the truth we never would have had the chance to fall in love, but now I want to tell you everything. I want to know you, Jane, and I want you to know me. I want to build a life with you." His smile was deep with yearning. "Nothing we do or say can change what happened. The only thing we can control is what we do with the here and now." His fingers curled into a fist, which he tapped against his palm. "I wish I could stand here and promise you that everything's going to work out. But I can't. Because I don't know what the future's going to dish up. I don't know if we'll have a day, a week, a decade, a lifetime together. It's what I want but I can't promise it." He sighed and cringed, running a hand through his hair as if he was annoyed at screwing up his speech.

I wanted to tell him to keep going, that he was doing great, but I couldn't speak.

"Look, all I can promise is to love you in every moment that I'm given. And right now, I want to marry you. And tomorrow, if we're lucky enough to wake up beside each other, I will cherish you then too…and the next day and the day after that. I will love you and care for you for as long as life gives me. I can say that with absolute conviction because you breathed life back into me and I can't live without you now." His voice wobbled. "I love you so much."

Tears were making it impossible to see. I slashed them off my cheeks and sniffed. Harry was still blurry, but I managed to see him grab the box off the bed and walk toward me. Dropping to one knee, he held up the ring.

"I know it's terrifying. Love is dangerous and it can tear you in half, but I think us together is worth that risk. So to hell with it, Janey. Let's jump into life together, eh? What do you say?"

It took a moment for me to swallow. I wiped a few more tears off my cheeks before giving him a wonky smile and whispering, "Geronimo."

His desperate expression dropped away and he gaped at me for a moment. "Geronimo?"

My head bobbed erratically. "Geronimo."

A wide smile burst across his face and he jumped up, grabbing me into a hug and spinning us around. "Geronimo!"

I laughed and cried, making these stupid whimpering sounds as he placed me down and slipped the ring on my shaky finger.

"It's Nan's," he murmured, his eyes shining as he smiled at me. "She wanted you to have it."

I touched the cluster of diamonds, cherishing how truly precious it was. The thought that his sweet grandmother had passed it on only intensified my tears.

Harry gently took my face and brushed the tears away with his thumbs before leaning down to kiss me.

His tender lips melted against mine and he murmured, "Geronimo" one more time before swiping his tongue into my mouth and reminding me of what home felt like.

I clutched his shoulders, diving into the kiss like it was the only thing I was born to do.

When he pulled back for air, I mumbled against his lips, "I love you. I love you."

We kissed some more, his hands gliding down my back and pulling me against him. I was getting ready to take things to the next level and christen the bed when the villa door burst open and Sarah hurried in.

"Oh, thank God." She tipped her head back and clapped her hands before pointing at Harry. "I told you, you had nothing to worry about."

He chuckled, still holding me tight as I leaned my cheek against his shoulder.

"Okay, let's get going." She flicked her fingers at me.

"What?" I frowned at my friend as Harry took a step back.

"We have so much to do. The wedding's at sunset. Come on, let's go."

"I'm sorry." I frowned at her. "I didn't realize you were expecting me to be your little helper!" I couldn't hide my terse tone. It may have been selfish, but I kind of had better things to do than rush around for some bride I didn't even know.

"I'm not." She giggled. "I'm expecting you to be the bride."

My breath hitched and I glanced at Harry. He winked at me then ran the back of his finger down my cheek. "You deserve a beautiful wedding, not a courthouse. But we knew you didn't want to have to plan one again."

"So, I did it for you. Trust me, it's going to be awesome!" Sarah sang, then grabbed my wrist and started tugging me out of the room.

I turned back to glance at Harry. His smile was like the sun as he mouthed, "See you soon."

All I could do was give him the same smile back as I was whisked away to get ready for my wedding.

THIRTY-SIX

HARRY

The grains of sand were cool beneath my feet. I stood there twitching as the cool breeze ruffled my curls. I was still in a mild state of shock that Jane had said yes. I guess I prepped myself for the big NO a little too well. At that moment, while I waited for my bride, I was caught in a surreal bubble. Sarah's brilliant surprise had paid off...and I was the luckiest man alive.

Justin and I had lit the torches that would guide Jane to my side. Behind me a guitarist I didn't know was tuning up for the *walk down the aisle* song. I had no idea what Sarah had chosen. Trying to coordinate it all from overseas had been slightly complicated, and in the end she told me to trust her and go with it.

All I really cared about was marrying Jane, so I gave in easily and followed all her instructions. When I arrived at the resort only a few hours before Jane, I was blown away by the luxury of it all, but Sarah told me her father owned a big record company and could afford to shell out for her best friend. My parents had paid for my flights as a wedding gift. I felt bad they couldn't be there, but in an effort to make Jane's wedding as un-wedding-ish as possible, we'd kept the guest list to only two witnesses—Sarah and Justin. I promised my parents a grand celebration over Christmas, then vowed to do the same for Jane's family over Thanksgiving. I was pretty sure her mother was in the throes of arranging a party as I stood on the beach waiting for my future wife.

Clearing my throat, I straightened the linen shirt Justin had brought to me a couple of hours earlier. It was white and I'd left the top two buttons undone and rolled up the sleeves. I looked like I was ready for a casual dinner by the poolside. Just the look Sarah was going for.

Justin tapped me on the shoulder. "Y-you good?"

"Yeah, mate. I'm feeling bloody tops right now." I nodded, and he gave me a little thumbs-up.

"This is r-right. If she's gonna marry anyone, i-it should be you."

I turned to him, my smile grateful as I extended

my hand. "Thank you. That means a lot. Sarah told me how close you were to your brother."

He shook my hand and nodded, then noticed something at the end of the beach. His eyebrows shot up, and he spun me back around before pointing at the guitarist.

The sun was setting behind me, lighting Jane's way with a golden beam. As she stepped into it, my breath hitched, my eyes welling with tears while the guitarist behind me started playing and singing, "Thinking Out Loud."

I couldn't take my watery gaze off her as she walked down the aisle with Sarah. Her red hair was curled and floating around her shoulders. A white flower was tucked behind her ear, pressed against her freckled cheek. Her dress was teal blue, reminding me of the waters from our European holiday. The soft fabric floated around her ankles, catching on the breeze and moving like its own ocean as she glided toward me. Pearl chains decorated her feet, wrapping around her big toes and up to her ankles. My eyes traveled back up her body again and over the fitted bodice that wound around her torso, culminating to a one-shoulder strap that was gathered with a neat line of pearls.

She looked breathtaking.

The song drew to a close just after she reached me. I took her hand and held it, gazing down at her with all the love and affection I possessed. It was a lot. I was overflowing with the emotion, my beaming smile testament to how much she owned my heart.

The celebrant's deep voice eased into our moment, guiding us through a simple ceremony that finished as the sky turned dark orange.

I kissed her under the night's first stars, treasuring the feel of her arms wrapping around my neck, her soft breath kissing my skin just before her lips did.

Sarah cheered while Justin clapped behind me, and I lifted Jane off her feet. She laughed into my mouth, then touched her nose against mine.

"I love you, Mr. Tindal."

"And I love you, my sweet Jane."

She smiled and kissed me again while the celebrant announced us husband and wife and the guitarist kicked in with another rendition of "Thinking Out Loud." It was the perfect song for the moment, and although I still had no idea how long I'd get to love the beautiful woman, I was confident that I would love her with everything, any chance I got.

My wife.

My beautiful Jane.

A love I would never take for granted.

*****

Jane glided across the bedroom floor, her teal dress still floating like water. It had been all night and I'd been mesmerized by it. I lay on the bed watching her. We were stuffed full of delicious food and slightly buzzed after one too many glasses of champagne. It had been the best night of my life. Watching Jane walk down the aisle toward me, hearing her declare she wanted to be mine…

I spun the simple gold band on my fourth finger and shook my head. I'd fought becoming a husband for so long, but maybe life had made me wait for Jane.

Who knew?

All I did understand with every fiber of my being was that the decisions I'd made throughout my day had been the right ones, and hopefully I could say that same thing tomorrow night.

"Come to bed, wifey." I patted the mattress.

Jane giggled and flicked her hair over her shoulder. "I will, I just have to give you something."

She pulled a booklet from her bag and walked over to me. With a mystified smile, I took it and studied the dragons on the front cover.

"Brandy wanted me to give it to you."

"She did this?"

Jane nodded.

I grinned and sat up, thumbing through the book while pride pulsed through me. That girl was a talent.

"It's amazing," I murmured, running my finger over the mended heart on the last page.

"She gave it to me just before she left for Chile. And then the principal walked in with that envelope from Sarah."

Setting the booklet aside, I turned to Jane and took her hand. "You didn't mind us surprising you?"

She tipped her head and let out a rueful chuckle. "As much as I hate surprises, I think it's sometimes the only way to bust through my stubborn veneer. I was so scared of losing you." She ran her fingers down my cheek. "I needed to see your face. The second I did, I knew I couldn't keep pretending. I may have found my way to a contented life eventually, but you make me so incredibly happy and I shouldn't deny myself that joy. Even if I only get it for another day."

I lightly held her wrist and kissed her palm. "Jane, we could have a lifetime of days ahead of us."

Her smile faltered like she couldn't quite believe it.

"It doesn't matter how many we get." I kissed her wrist. "Let's just live one day at time and make the most of it."

"I like the sound of that." Her smile grew wide and beautiful.

I leaned forward and kissed it, gently pushing her onto the bed so I could cover her with my body. Working my way across her cheek, I kissed her neck and down across her bare shoulder. She let out a blissful sigh, running her fingers into my hair and whispering, "You've added so many things to my list today."

I looked up at her and grinned. "Do you have it with you? We could write them on and cross them off."

She giggled then wrinkled her nose. "I haven't touched the list since you left LA."

"Well, that won't do." My eyebrows knit together.

Her eyes sparkled as she brushed her teeth over her bottom lip. "Do you want to start a new one? We could call it 'Jane and Harry's To Do List.'"

"Or…" I lightly nipped her shoulder, then gave her a cheeky wink. "We could call it 'Jane and Harry's Done It List.'" Gliding my hand down her leg, I gathered the soft material with my fingers, sliding it up until I could reach her smooth skin. Palming her thigh, I traveled up to her perfect bottom and gave it a gentle squeeze.

She chuckled and hooked her leg over my thigh, giving me full access to her delectable arse.

"Let's stop making a list of wishes and start writing down everything we've achieved instead. We know what it's like to lose. We know the importance of making life count. Adding to our list each day will be a reminder that we're not wasting our lives, that we're living in the moment and cherishing all it has to offer."

Her eyes glittered like fireflies as she pressed her body against mine and kissed me. Rubbing her thumb over my bottom lip, she smiled and whispered, "You want to add something to the list right now?"

"If that hungry look in your eye is saying what I think it is, then most definitely."

She laughed and wriggled out of my grasp. "Come on, then."

"Where are you going?" I rolled over to watch her run around the bed. She stopped in the doorway and unhooked the strap of her dress. My body stirred with desire at the sound of her zipper coming undone. Wriggling her hips, she shimmied out of the dress then whipped her knickers off.

"Aphrodite," I whispered with a smile.

Her cheeks flamed with color as I openly admired her. "I've always wanted to make love in the water. Fancy a midnight dip in the pool?"

I was ripping off my shirt before she'd even finished talking. As soon as my pants hit the floor, I walked across the room naked and swept her into my arms. Carrying her through the villa, we stepped into the tropical night air. I stopped at the edge of the pool and smiled down at her moonlit face.

"Geronimo, sweet Jane."

She wrapped her arms around my neck and squealed as I jumped into the water. The second our heads popped above the surface, our lips met in a wet, frenetic kiss that rivaled our first reunion. Her legs wrapped around my hips and I walked her to the edge of the pool, where I happily added the first item to our list.

It was a magical moment listening to Jane's sweet moans, her milky skin cast in moonlight while the stars twinkled above us. The water blanketed us as I came inside her, sealing our marriage vows and opening the next chapter of our lives.

I had no idea what would be written on each page, but I was determined to fill them with as many good things as I possibly could.

Life was for living, loving, appreciating…and Jane and I were going to prove it.

EPILOGUE

JANE

"I'll see you guys tomorrow. Don't forget to bring in your book assignments!" I called to my class as they filtered out the door.

The final bell for the day had just rung, and I was pretty sure none of them heard me.

Most of them were still trying to get back into the swing after the Christmas/New Year break. Gearing them up to think again was always challenging. I grinned and shook my head. I didn't blame them. It was hard to get down to work when there was always something better waiting outside of school. My cheeks heated with color. As much as

I loved my job, I was no longer obsessed with it. I didn't need to be. Harry made life worth embracing, and I'd learned to switch off the second I left the building.

I checked my watch and tried to calculate how long it would take me to set up for the next day's classes. If I worked fast enough I could beat rush hour and get home to my husband that much quicker. Unless I just left it and came in early the next morning.

That was appealing.

"See ya, Mrs. Tindal."

"Bye, sweetie." I waved to Annie as she walked out the door. That's when I noticed Troy hovering in the hallway. As soon as Annie turned down the corridor, he stepped into my room.

"Good afternoon, Mr. Baker." I crossed my arms and grinned. "To what do I owe the pleasure of this visit?"

He chuckled. "Maybe I just wanted to swing by and see that smile again."

I blushed.

"No, seriously. It gives me hope." He perched his butt on the corner of my desk. "Since you've been married, you've had a complete transformation. You suit being Mrs. Tindal."

"Well, it's lucky I love it so much, then."

He grinned, but his smile soon fled as he placed a manila folder on my desk. "We've got a new kid coming in. He's a…" Troy scratched his forehead, his eyebrows popping up as he looked at the folder with a sad smile. "It's a bit of a tragic story. His mother died recently and he's moved in with his estranged aunt who is completely out of her depth. She doesn't seem to want him, but she's also adamant that he can't go into foster care. Poor thing's only twenty-two, and she's really struggling."

"How old's her nephew?"

"He turned twelve last week."

"Whoa," I muttered, reaching for the file. Flipping it open, I read the name—Felix Grayson. He had big brown eyes, much like Brandy's, and a mop of thick, wayward hair.

"He keeps getting into fights at his current school. They want to kick him out, so I've stepped in and scored him a scholarship here."

"Don't you think he'll just get into fights here?"

"Sometimes a change of scenery can do wonders. I can't help wondering if most of those fights were simply self-defense. I've had a few sessions with him, but he won't talk to me. I don't think he's a bad kid. I think he's just scared and misses his mom. He's really quiet and doesn't give off aggressive vibes, but I don't think he's the type to just sit back and take a beating either."

"Father?"

Troy shook his head. "There's no name listed on his birth certificate."

I scanned his school records, noting his higher grades at elementary school and the serious drop-off when he hit fifth grade. "Was his mother sick before she died?"

"Yeah, she was diagnosed with cancer just after

he turned ten."

I winced, hurting for the poor boy already. "So, I take it he'll be in my homeroom."

"Yeah, plus English. He starts next week."

"Okay." I nodded. "Well, thanks for the heads-up. I'll try to help him if I can."

"You did such a great job helping Brandy, I actually requested that he go into your class."

I smiled, my cheeks tinging red again. "I didn't—"

"You did." He cut me off. "And you will again. Hopefully between me and his teachers we can help this kid get through." Troy sighed. "I get the impression he and his mom were pretty tight. She was his everything and now she's gone, you know?"

"Yeah." I nodded. "I do know."

Troy's lips pushed into a smile. "Which is why I requested you. He needs someone to show him that it's okay to move on and find joy without his mom. I doubt his struggling aunt's going to be able to revive him, so it's up to us."

"Well, I'll give it my best shot."

"You're a first-class case of reviving a life, Jane." He walked for the door. "It gives me hope!" he called over his shoulder, then stopped and smiled at something to his right. Spinning back, he wiggled his eyebrows at my bemused expression and said, "Have a good night."

As soon as he started walking away, a bunch of red roses appeared in my doorway, followed by my husband who was singing "I Love You Too

Much."

I giggled when he did a twirl, his voice crescendo-ing into the second verse. Using the bouquet as a microphone, he swayed from side to side, serenading me with his true Harry charm.

Taking my hand, he pulled me against his chest and waltzed me between the desks, grinning and singing until he reached the end. Tipping me back, he whispered the last line then kissed me softly on the lips.

My smile was broad and enchanted. We'd only been married three months, and I found it funny how some days it felt like a lifetime and other days it felt like we'd only just started dating. Harry made me feel so comfortable, yet I still got those giddy buzzes shooting through my system whenever he smiled at me or held me close.

Swinging me back up to standing, he tucked my bangs behind my ear and, with a flourish, handed me the slightly bruised roses.

"For you, Mrs. Tindal."

"Why, thank you." I laughed, taking the bouquet and sniffing the petals. "What's the occasion?"

"Do I need an occasion?" He pulled me to his side and pecked my nose.

"Hmm, I guess not."

"Well, why don't we make it one?"

"Meaning?"

He twirled me under his arm then guided me toward my desk. "Let's go home and fancy up for some classy dinner. I could take you to that new place near your parents' house. What's it called again?"

"Vincenzo's."

"Yes!" He clicked his fingers. "Vincenzo's it is."

I slid my computer into my bag and ignored my planning folder. It could wait until the morning. Harry took the bag from me and started for the door, but I stopped him with another suggestion.

"Or…" My eyes gleamed as I plucked a red petal from the bunch and ran it beneath my nose then across my lips. "We could just go home and make love on a bed of rose petals."

His smile was slow and sexy as he hitched my bag onto his shoulder and retraced his steps. "Well, you know I only have one thing to say about that."

He sidled up against me, nuzzling my neck until I started giggling then whispered into his ear, "Geronimo?"

"You better bloody believe it." He swept me off the floor.

I laughed and held tight as he walked me out of the school and straight for my car. We still lived in my tiny studio apartment. We were saving for a new place, but for now the little apartment was ours and it was home.

Home.

I loved that word.

Harry had made it real to me once more. When I woke each morning and found him lying beside me, I was filled with an overwhelming sense of comfort and gratitude. If tragedy had taught me anything, it was to cherish each moment I was given. And Harry had the ability to make each and every moment magical. As I fingered the rose petals on my lap, I glanced at my husband and smiled.

He winked at me and continued to drive us home. His wedding ring caught my eye, the simple gold band on his fourth finger making him mine. Giddy love bubbles rose within me, popping and bursting as I grinned out the window.

Yes, love was a risk.

But it was a beautiful one, and I'd be forever grateful I took a leap of faith and jumped back into it.

I was the happiest version of myself that I'd ever been, and although no one could guarantee me a lifetime of it, I'd cherish each and every second I got.

THE END

Thank you so much for reading *Geronimo*. If you've enjoyed it and would like to show me some support, please consider leaving an honest review.

KEEP READING TO FIND OUT ABOUT THE NEXT SONGBIRD NOVEL...

The next Songbird Novel belongs to:

Troy, Cassie, & Felix

HOLE-HEARTED

Is due for release in Autumn 2016

Cassie Grayson doesn't know how to be a mom. She's twenty-two and hardly in a position to care for a kid. But when her twelve-year-old nephew is dumped in her lap, she does the only thing she can: she takes him in.

Neither of them have it easy as they try to navigate this unknown path. Cassie must deal with her feelings toward her estranged sister and her own rocky childhood growing up in the foster care system. Felix is still reeling from being uprooted from the only life he's ever known, and he doesn't quite connect with his weird, emotionless aunt. The only person he thinks might be mildly okay is Troy Baker, the counselor at his new school.

To Troy, Felix and Cassie should be just another case, but they're not. Something about the hopeless duo captures his heart, and in spite of his hesitation he finds himself falling for both of them. Felix's quiet strength is endearing, but it's Cassie's determination to overcome the demons from her past that chips away at his own walls, daring him to heal her…and maybe, just maybe, fall in love.

Can three strangers from completely different worlds create an unlikely family? Or are the holes in their hearts too big to heal?

SPECIAL OFFER
If you'd like to receive the exclusive Songbird novella — Angel Eyes — plus some extra bonuses for newsletter subscribers only, you can follow this link to find out more:
http://eepurl.com/1cqdj

You can find the other Songbird Novels on Amazon.

FEVER
Ella & Cole's story

BULLETPROOF
Morgan & Sean's story

EVERYTHING
Jody & Leo's story

HOME
Rachel & Josh's story

TRUE LOVE
Nessa & Jimmy's story

TROUBLEMAKER
Marcus & Kelly's story

ROUGH WATER
Justin & Sarah's story

.

NOTE FROM THE AUTHOR

One of the things I loved most about writing *Geronimo* was Jane and Harry's trip through Europe—the spontaneous adventure of throwing all caution to the wind and just experiencing life. I am such a planner. I don't like things being thrown at me and I'm not good at just impulsively doing things. I need to learn to live in the moment more, and it was good for me to write a story that forced my characters to do just that. Life can sometimes be hell, but it can also be beautiful, and stopping to notice even simple things like the warmth of the sun on your skin or the sound of someone's laughter can make your life more meaningful, and get you through those darker moments.

I hope I have given you *a happy moment* while you've read this story. As always, I hope it made you feel...and I hope it made you fall in love. The soundtrack is one of my favorites and I have listened to the playlist MANY times while writing the book. The songs are embedded in my heart and make me think of Harry and Jane every time I hear them.

Thank you so much for reading this Songbird ovel. I can't tell you how much of a privilege it is to produce these stories. There are only two more left, plus a couple of Chaos novellas. It's going to be really weird finishing the collection, but I'm also excited for the things ahead. Thanks for walking this journey with me. It wouldn't be the same without my lovely readers.

xx
Melissa

Keep reading for the playlist and the link to find it on Spotify.

GERONIMO SOUNDTRACK

(Please note: The songs listed below are not always the original versions, but the ones I chose to listen to while constructing this book. The songs are listed in the order they appear.)

A THOUSAND YEARS
Performed by Christina Perri

BE MORE BARRIO
Performed by Sheppard

GERONIMO
Performed by Sheppard

BEST DAY OF MY LIFE
Performed by American Authors

THE EDGE OF GLORY
Performed by Walk Off The Earth

KISS ME
Performed by Ed Sheeran

CAN'T STOP THE FEELING
Performed by Justin Timberlake

OVER THE RAINBOW
Performed by Israel Kamakawiwo'ole

MELISSA PEARL

TO MAKE YOU FEEL MY LOVE
Performed by Elvis Blue

EVERY LITTLE THING SHE DOES IS MAGIC
Performed by The Police

WHEREVER YOU GO
Performed by Ron Pope

ON TOP OF THE WORLD
Performed by Imagine Dragons

FIREFLIES
Performed by Owl City

COUNTING STARS
Performed by OneRepublic

ODDS ARE
Performed by Barenaked Ladies

GONNA WALK
Performed by Barenaked Ladies

SOMEBODY TO YOU
Performed by The Vamps

THE LUCKIEST
Performed by Ben Folds

UNSTEADY
Performed by X Ambassadors

IT'S SO HARD TO SAY GOODBYE TO
YESTERDAY
Performed by Jason Mraz

SAY
Performed by John Mayer

SEE YOU SOMEDAY
Performed by Forty Foot Echo

YOU MATTER TO ME
Performed by Sara Bareilles & Jason Mraz

MARRY ME
Performed by Train

IT'S GOOD (IT'S NOT SAFE)
Performed by Sidewalk Prophets

THINKING OUT LOUD
Performed by Ed Sheeran

I LOVE YOU TOO MUCH
Performed by Gustavo Santaolalla, Deigo Luna

**To enhance your reading experience, you can
listen along to the playlist for GERONIMO on
Spotify:
https://open.spotify.com/user/12146962946/play
list/7d6YqfyXi2TolU5qUzcPNY**

ACKNOWLEDGEMENTS

Thank you so much to everyone who had input in producing *Geronimo*.

My critique readers: Cassie and Rae. Your enthusiasm was magical. Thank you so much for making the book what it is now.

My editor: Laurie. You are so incredibly brilliant to work with.

My proofreaders: I love you guys. Thank you for your time and attention.

My advanced reading team: What would I do without you? Thank you so much for your constant support and enthusiasm.

My cover designer and photographer: Regina. I saw the cover image months ago and earmarked it for Jane and Harry's story. It's the perfect shot and you made it into the perfect cover.

My fellow writers: Inklings and Indie Inked. I love that after all this time, I can still check in with you guys for advice and encouragement.

My fan club and readers: You guys are seriously the best! You keep me flying and I'm so, so grateful.

My gorgeous husband: Thanks for being so easy to live with. Being with you is the most natural thing in the world. It's as easy as breathing and I love you for it. Thanks for introducing me to BNL too. I think of you every time I hear one of their songs.

My family: You guys are my sunshine. Thanks for the cuddles, the love and your constant believe in me.

My maker: Thank you for filling my life with moments and teaching me how to be grateful. You have given me so much. I'll love you forever.

OTHER BOOKS BY MELISSA PEARL

The Songbird Novels
Fever—Bulletproof—Everything—Home—True
Love—Troublemaker—Rough Water—Geronimo
Coming in autumn 2016: Hole-Hearted

The Space Between Heartbeats
Plus two novellas: The Space Before & The Space
Beyond

The Fugitive Series
I Know Lucy — Set Me Free

The Masks Series
True Colors — Two-Faced— Snake Eyes — Poker
Face

The Time Spirit Trilogy
Golden Blood — Black Blood — Pure Blood

The Elements Trilogy
Unknown — Unseen — Unleashed

The Mica & Lexy Series
Forbidden Territory—Forbidden Waters

Find out more on Melissa Pearl's website:
www.melissapearlauthor.com

CPSIA information can be obtained
at www.ICGtesting.com
Printed in the USA
LVOW11s0248161116
513165LV00001B/52/P